O9-AID-545

Dial "R" for Revenge . . .

Deena was drifting off to sleep when the ringing phone jarred her awake.

"Hello?" she murmured, her voice clogged with sleep.

"Deena? Deena Martinson?" the voice on the other end whispered.

"Who is this?" Deena demanded, sitting up, her heart pounding.

"Let's just say I'm an old friend. Someone you haven't seen in a long time."

"What do you want?" Deena cried shrilly.

"Revenge," the voice whispered.

Deena heard a click. The line went dead.

Books by R. L. Stine

Available from ARCHWAY Paperbacks

For orders other than by individual consumers, Archway Books grants a discount on the purchase of **10 or more** copies of single titles for special markets or premium use. For further details, please write to the Vice-President of Special Markets, Pocket Books, 1230 Avenue of the Americas, New York, NY 10020.

For information on how individual consumers can place orders, please write to Mail Order Department, Paramount Publishing, 200 Old Tappan Road, Old Tappan, NJ 07675.

FEAR STREET®

R·L·STINE

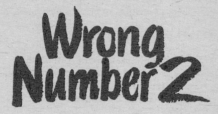

Wrong Number 2

A Parachute Press Book

AN ARCHWAY PAPERBACK
Published by POCKET BOOKS
New York   London   Toronto   Sydney   Tokyo   Singapore

The sale of this book without its cover is unauthorized. If you purchased
this book without a cover, you should be aware that it was reported to
the publisher as "unsold and destroyed." Neither the author nor the
publisher has received payment for the sale of this "stripped book."

This book is a work of fiction. Names, characters, places and
incidents are products of the author's imagination or are used
fictitiously. Any resemblance to actual events or locales or persons,
living or dead, is entirely coincidental.

AN ARCHWAY PAPERBACK *Original*

An Archway Paperback published by
POCKET BOOKS, a division of Simon & Schuster Inc.
1230 Avenue of the Americas, New York, NY 10020

Copyright © 1995 by Parachute Press, Inc.

All rights reserved, including the right to reproduce
this book or portions thereof in any form whatsoever.
For information address Pocket Books, 1230 Avenue
of the Americas, New York, NY 10020

ISBN: 0-671-78607-5

First Archway Paperback printing January 1995

10 9 8 7 6 5 4 3 2 1

FEAR STREET is a registered trademark of
Parachute Press, Inc.

AN ARCHWAY PAPERBACK and colophon are
registered trademarks of Simon & Schuster Inc.

Cover art by Bill Schmidt

Printed in the U.S.A.

IL 7+

prologue

The grinding roar of the chain saw grew louder. Its jarring vibrations made the entire tree shake.

Desperately, Deena clung to the high tree branch. Next to her, Jade, her features twisted in horror, wrapped her arms tightly around the trunk and held on.

The tree began to shake harder as the chains bit through the thick bark and into the wood. Struggling frantically not to slip off, Deena stared down through the night darkness into the determined face of Stanley Farberson.

"No!" she screamed. "No—please!"

But the screech of the chain saw drowned out her pleas.

Farberson killed his wife. And now he's going to kill Jade and me because we know what he did!

The terrifying thought repeated in her mind. Repeated until the words roared louder than the grinding saw.

The tree shook more violently. Deena heard a frightening *crack.*

The sound of bones breaking, she thought.

The trunk split. And then the whole tree began to tilt.

"We're going down!" Jade wailed. Then said nothing more, her face frozen in a mask of terror.

Deena hugged the branch tighter as the tree started to topple. She opened her mouth to scream—but no sound came out.

Her eyes bulging in horror, she watched as the tree began to fall, carrying her with it.

And now she was falling—falling straight into the whirling blades of the saw.

"Ohh." Deena let out a low moan and shook her head.

"I'm okay." Yes, she was okay. She was hunched over her desk, staring at the night sky outside her bedroom window.

Remembering.

Remembering once again that horrifying night. The night on Fear Street. The night Stanley Farberson nearly killed her and Jade.

A year has passed, she told herself, shaking her head

2

as if trying to shake away the memories. Why do I keep reliving it again and again? Why do I keep putting myself back in that tree, watching Farberson's wild eyes, hearing the roar of the chain saw.

Deena stood up and walked shakily to the dresser mirror. Leaning on the dresser, she gazed at herself, at her tired eyes, her tense, tight-lipped expression.

"There's nothing to be afraid of now," she told herself. "Farberson is in prison. Locked up for life. He can't get out. He can't hurt us now. He can't . . ."

chapter

1

"So how would I look as a blonde?"

"What?" Deena Martinson slammed her history book shut and gazed up at her friend.

"I'm serious," Jade Smith said, twirling a strand of her long auburn hair around her finger. "I think being blond would be interesting, don't you? I'd look just like Sharon Stone."

Deena laughed. "I don't believe you," she said. "You have the most beautiful hair in the school, and you want to change it?"

"Or maybe I should get colored contacts." Jade rolled off her bed, where she'd been studying. She stood in front of her full-length mirror. Her bright green cat suit made her eyes appear even greener, and showed off her great figure.

She curled her thumbs and forefingers into little *O*'s and held them around her eyes. "How would I look with blue eyes?" she asked.

"Jade, what's your problem?" Deena demanded. "You're totally gorgeous the way you are. Why do you want to change anything?"

"I'm bored," Jade complained. She dropped back on her bed, fished around in the night-table drawer for an emery board, and began to file the nails on her left hand.

"So am I," Deena said, sighing. "Maybe *I'm* the one who should get a new look."

"Why do you say that?" asked Jade.

"I don't know. Maybe it would be easier to find a new boyfriend if I looked different."

Jade laughed. "What's the story with you and Pete Goodwin?"

"Pete's kind of boring," Deena replied softly.

"You want to get back with Rob Morell—don't you!" Jade accused.

Deena could feel her face getting hot and knew she was blushing. "Maybe."

"Well, forget it," Jade told her. "Rob is so stoked over Debra Kern, he can barely speak to anyone else." Jade concentrated on her nails. "What about Steve Mason? He's kind of cute. And he has that great Australian accent."

"He'd never be interested in me," Deena murmured.

"Why not?" Jade asked. "All you have to do is go after him."

"For sure!" Deena said, rolling her eyes. "And how am I supposed to do that?"

"It's easy," Jade replied. "The next time you see him, just go up and talk to him. Let him know you're interested."

"Why would that make him interested in me?"

"It always works for me," Jade said. "In fact—"

The phone on her night table rang. She set down the emery board to pick up the receiver. "Oh, *hi*, Teddy!" Her voice sounded as if it were dripping with honey. "Well, of course I do. How are you?"

Deena stared at her friend in awe. When she spoke to a boy, Jade's whole face changed. Her eyes lit up, and her mouth twisted into a mischievous smile. The tone of her voice made it sound as if the boy were the most wonderful person in the whole world.

Deena and Jade had been friends since fourth grade. But Deena still didn't know how her friend managed to do it.

"Yes, Teddy, we will. Uh-huh. That's Friday night, right? Of course. Wouldn't miss it. Okay." Jade hung up the phone.

"Teddy, right?" Deena asked.

"Uh-huh." Jade nodded. "He wanted to make sure I'm going to the game tomorrow night."

Teddy Miller, the star guard for the Shadyside Tigers basketball team, was tall and rugged. Most of the girls thought he was one of the best-looking guys in the school. He'd gone out with at least a dozen girls, and now he was very interested in Jade.

"Hey, I thought you and I were going to the game together," Deena said.

"Well, of course we're going together," Jade replied. "Teddy just wants to make sure I watch him play." She narrowed her eyes and studied Deena. "You know what's wrong with you?" she said. "You don't have enough confidence."

Deena laughed. "What does that have to do with anything?"

"That's why you won't go up and talk to Steve," Jade concluded. "You're one of the cutest and smartest girls at Shadyside High. I don't know why you won't let Steve know that."

Because I'm shy, Deena thought to herself. But then she realized that was just another way of saying she didn't have confidence. Maybe Jade was right.

"Hand me my brush, will you?" asked Jade. "It's on the dresser."

Deena reached for the hairbrush. Underneath it was an envelope addressed to Jade. She handed Jade the brush, then picked up the envelope. Deena recognized the handwriting. "Is this from Chuck?" she asked.

"It came yesterday," Jade said, running the brush through her auburn hair.

"How often does he write you?" Deena asked.

"Every week," Jade replied.

"You're kidding!" Deena cried. "Chuck has time at college to write letters?"

"Guess so," Jade said.

"Maybe college has changed him," Deena said thoughtfully, staring at the envelope. "He seems to be keeping out of trouble. Not one call from the police down there!"

Jade snickered. "Your half brother is a wild man, all right! I think he's the most hotheaded guy I ever met." She continued brushing out her hair.

Hotheaded is *one* word for it, Deena thought darkly. *Crazy* is another. But maybe Chuck has learned to control that temper of his.

She felt the memories of last year pushing their way back into her mind. She remembered Chuck making those stupid phone calls. Calling phone numbers at random—just for laughs.

But the laughs had ended when Chuck dialed the number on Fear Street. Stanley Farberson's number. Chuck had called at a bad time. Farberson was about to murder his wife. Her screams in the background forced Deena, Jade, and Chuck to go to their house to investigate.

To get involved.

To get involved in a horrible murder. To nearly get themselves killed too.

All because of Chuck.

"Sometimes he writes more often," Jade said. "He's really become kind of sweet. Too bad I don't have time to answer."

"What do you mean you don't have time?" Deena accused.

"You know I like Chuck," Jade explained. "But, really, he's off in college, and I'm here in Shadyside. Am I supposed to pine away for him?"

Deena didn't answer for a moment. Jade always went from boy to boy. But somehow it made a difference when it was Deena's own half brother. "Does Chuck know you're going out with Teddy? And the other guys?" Deena asked.

"I don't know *what* Chuck knows," Jade answered sharply. "I mean, what Chuck doesn't know can't hurt him, right?"

"I guess," Deena muttered. She felt annoyed. It wasn't as if Jade and Chuck were engaged or anything. But it seemed to Deena that they were right for each other.

"If Chuck finds out and loses his temper—" Deena started to say.

"No problem. I can handle Chuck," Jade assured her. She finished brushing her hair and stood up. "I'm going to get some chips or something downstairs. Want a Coke?" she asked.

Without waiting for an answer, Jade started down the hall. As she did, the phone rang again. "Would you get that for me?" she called back.

"Sure," Deena said. She picked up the phone. As a goof, she decided to try to imitate Jade's honey-dripping voice. "Hellooooo," she purred.

"Is this Jade?" the voice on the other end growled.

"Who *is* this?" Deena asked, her heart pounding.

"This is your wrong number, Jade," the deep voice rasped.

"Huh? My what?"

"This is your wrong number. I'm coming to disconnect your line. Real soon."

chapter
2

"Who was it?" Jade asked, walking back into the room. She set a bowl of chips on the dresser and handed Deena a can of Coke.

"It was— I think it was a wrong number," Deena stammered.

"I get a lot of wrong numbers," Jade said, chewing on a large potato chip. "I wonder if—" She stopped when she saw Deena's expression. "Deena? You look weird. Is something wrong?"

"It was the call," Deena explained. "He said he was your—your wrong number."

"What's that supposed to mean?"

"Jade, it sounded like Mr. Farberson!" Deena cried. "His voice was all deep and hoarse."

"You're kidding," Jade said, surprisingly calm. She

reached for another handful of chips. "It couldn't be him, Deena. No way."

"I know," Deena admitted. "But he had the same kind of scary voice. And he said—he was coming here or something."

"No way," Jade repeated. "Farberson was sentenced to twenty years. He won't even be up for parole for years."

"Well . . ." Deena thought about it a moment. "You're right. I know you are. But I can't help being upset whenever I think about him. I still have nightmares about what happened."

"So do I," Jade admitted. "I mean, he nearly killed us, after all.

"It's hard to believe it all started with a phone call," Jade continued.

"A *prank* call," Deena added. "But it was so much fun—at least at first."

"I loved it when we were calling up those guys," Jade said, grinning. "Remember putting on those sexy voices and trying to convince them we were secretly in love with them? What a crazy thing to do."

"But it stopped being fun once Chuck got involved," Deena reminded her. "Especially when he started making threatening calls."

"Chuck is a baaaad dude," Jade said, snickering. She offered Deena the bowl of chips. "That call you just answered was probably some jerk from school trying to scare us. After all, everyone in Shadyside knows what happened last year."

13

"Yeah. Probably," Deena replied thoughtfully. "But it was still kind of frightening."

"Forget about it," Jade said firmly. "Here. Have some potato chips. Live dangerously!"

Deena's call came a little before midnight.

She had just turned out the light and was drifting off to sleep. The ringing phone jarred her awake.

"Hello?" she murmured, her voice clogged with sleep.

"Deena? Deena Martinson?" the voice on the other end whispered.

"Yes?" Fear rushed in.

"I called your friend earlier," the voice rasped.

"Who is this?" Deena demanded, sitting up, her heart pounding.

"Let's just say I'm an old friend. Someone you haven't seen for a long time."

"What do you want?" Deena cried shrilly.

She suddenly felt angry. It *couldn't* be Farberson. He was in prison. So who was making these calls?

"What do you *want?*" Deena shouted.

"Revenge," the voice whispered.

Deena heard a click. The line went dead.

The next morning Deena struggled to pay attention in algebra, but she couldn't get her mind to concentrate on numbers. Instead, she kept hearing the caller's rough voice, and the frightening one-word threat— *"Revenge."*

Deena was taken completely by surprise when Mr. Forrest handed out a review quiz. She didn't have a chance to complete it by the time the bell rang. So she quickly scribbled answers to the last three problems.

She handed in her quiz and began gathering her papers and books. As she headed through the door, she nearly bumped into Steve Mason. He had a class in that room next period.

The trouble with you is you don't have any confidence. Jade's words from the night before rang in her mind. *Just talk to him,* Jade had instructed. *Let him know you're interested.*

Why not? Deena thought. Before she could think twice about it, she made herself talk to him. "Hi, Steve!" She greeted him with a big smile.

"Hey. G'day," he replied, surprised.

"How do you like the cold weather?" Deena blurted out.

"It's not bad, actually," he said. "Different from Sydney." He smiled at her.

"Who's Sydney?" Deena joked.

She expected him to laugh, but he didn't.

Does he think I don't know that Sydney is a city in Australia? Deena wondered, feeling her face grow red.

"Well, have a nice day," she finished lamely. What a *bomb!* she thought unhappily, hurrying away.

"Yeah. Bye now," she heard him call after her.

* * *

When Deena came out of gym, her last class, she found Jade waiting for her by the water fountain. Jade was wearing a bright red cat suit with a short black jacket.

I could never wear anything like that, Deena thought. But Jade, as usual, looked fabulous.

Also, as usual, she was surrounded by boys— Teddy and three of his friends from the basketball team.

"Talk to you later, Teddy." Jade gave him a big smile. "Deena and I are going to my house to work on our science term papers."

"Later," Teddy said, giving both girls a quick one-fingered salute. He ambled off with his friends.

Deena led the way out of school. A bright sun peeked through puffs of cloud, but the air felt cold. Snow had been on the ground for several days. Now it was patchy and gray. The sidewalks were puddled and covered with dirty slush.

Jade's house wasn't far from school. As they walked down Park Drive, Deena began telling her friend about the midnight phone call.

"You're kidding!" Jade exclaimed. "The same guy?"

"It sounded like him," Deena insisted. "He called me by my name, and he mentioned you."

"It's got to be some jerk playing a dumb joke— right?" Jade asked. "No way it could be Farberson." She sounded a little uncertain. "People can't sit around in their prison cells making phone calls, right?"

"I don't think so," said Deena. "But even if Farberson could, why would he call us? He's going to be in there for years and years."

"So it's *got* to be someone else. Someone who wants to give us a scare," Jade decided.

"I guess."

"That means the best way to deal with it is to not be scared," Jade suggested.

"Right," Deena echoed. She started to tell Jade about her very short conversation with Steve that morning—when her friend suddenly grabbed her wrist.

"Deena!" Jade whispered. "Do you see that car up ahead?"

Deena hadn't been paying attention, but now she turned to the street. A battered green Oldsmobile with tinted windows was slowly cruising away from them. "What about it?" she said.

"It just passed us for the second time."

"You're kidding," said Deena. "Why would it do that? Is it someone from school?"

"I don't know. But I wonder— There it goes." The car abruptly sped up and turned the corner, its tires squealing.

"Weird," Jade murmured. "Anyway, what were you about to say?"

Deena gathered her scattered thoughts and told

Jade what had happened that morning when she'd run into Steve. "He didn't even get my joke!" she wailed.

Jade laughed. "Maybe he heard it before." Her expression turned serious. "So what happened after you talked to him?"

"Nothing."

"Nothing?"

"Well, I had to go to class. Besides, I didn't know what else to say."

"It doesn't matter what you say," Jade assured her. "Just keep letting him know you're interested. Next time you see him, ask him about something. Ask him about his favorite Australian rock band. Or ask him what sports he played back home. Just don't make any more jokes about Sydney."

"But I don't know anything—" Deena stopped as a car drew alongside the two girls. "Jade—it's the same car!"

"I see it," Jade whispered. The beat-up car was a deep, muddy green, with windows tinted so dark it was impossible to see who was inside.

"Just ignore it," Jade instructed. The car was barely crawling now, keeping pace with the girls.

They began to walk a little faster, and the car sped up.

Deena squinted to see the driver. But the dark-tinted windows acted as a shield.

Jade stopped abruptly. The car stopped too.

"Jade, come on," Deena said breathlessly. "Let's get *out* of here."

Jade turned to face the car. At the same time, Deena heard the click of a car door opening.

"Jade—" she cried in panic. "He—he's coming after us!"

"Run!" Jade yelled.

chapter
3

Jade grabbed Deena's arm and tugged her over the patchy snow. They ducked into an opening between two houses.

Was he following them? Was he right behind them?

The girls were too afraid to turn back. Slipping through soft ice and mud, they ran down a narrow, twisting alleyway.

By the time the concrete wall that surrounded Jade's yard appeared, Deena was struggling to breathe. A sharp pain stabbed at her side.

"Come on!" Jade gasped, pulling open the gate.

Panting, Deena ducked inside to the safety of the yard.

Jade slammed the gate. Then, sucking in deep

breaths, she poked her head over it and peered back the way they had come. "No one there," she reported.

"But that car was *definitely* following us," Jade insisted, still breathing hard.

"Maybe the person just wanted directions," Deena suggested, waiting for the pain in her side to fade.

"Maybe," said Jade. "But I don't really believe that—and I don't think you do either."

"You don't think it was the same person who made the phone calls, do you?" Deena asked.

"I—I don't know what to think," her friend stammered. "But I don't want to take any chances. Let's go inside."

The next day, Friday, her frightening run down the alley lingered in Deena's mind as she made her way through the halls of Shadyside High.

Steve Mason, where are you? she wondered to herself.

She had decided to try to talk to him again. But she hadn't seen him all day.

Was he out sick?

No. Turning a corner, Deena caught a glimpse of him going into the science lab. He wasn't alone.

He was walking with Bree Wade, one of the tall, dark-haired Wade twins. They were walking close together and sharing a laugh.

Of course! Deena thought bitterly. Why did I ever think I could go after a boy the way Jade does?

Forget about Steve, she told herself. And that's just what she tried to do all during the volleyball game in gym. She was drying her fine, short blond hair after class, when she noticed Jade standing behind her in the mirror.

"Oh, hi, Jade." Deena gave a last blast of hot air to her bangs and set the dryer down.

"If we're going to get to the game to watch them practice, we have to hurry," Jade said. "The bell rang ten minutes ago."

Right. The game. Deena slid the dryer into her backpack and slung the pack and her overnight bag over her shoulder. Her parents were going to a concert in Waynesbridge, so Deena was going to Jade's to spend the night after the game.

They dropped their gear at Jade's, then took a bus to Mattewan High. They arrived in time to get fifth row seats at center court.

Deena had never really liked basketball, but she loved going to games. She loved to see all her friends and to cheer the Shadyside players.

"Hi, Deena! Hi, Jade!" It was Lisa Blume, carrying a big bag of popcorn. "Great seats, guys!"

"See?" said Jade. "I told you it pays to come early."

"Yeah, maybe," said Deena. But she knew the real reason Jade liked to come early—to watch the guys warm up.

Most of the rows were filling up. Jade made her way down to the floor to say hello to Teddy. Deena let her eyes wander around the crowded stands.

Steve—are you here? she wondered.

No sign of him.

Maybe he doesn't like American sports, she thought. Or maybe he's sitting on the wrong side. After all, he hadn't been in the States that long. Maybe he didn't know about home and visiting teams.

She glanced across the court to the home team seats. The bleachers were a sea of red and blue, Mattewan's colors. She'd never find Steve if he was over there.

Deena was about to give up—when someone caught her eye. A man wearing an orange hunting cap slouched in the shadows at the side of the bleachers.

His cap was pulled down so far she couldn't see his face. There was something strange about him, but something familiar too.

"Teddy's such a great guy," Jade said, scooting back in beside Deena. "He says we're going to win. What are you staring at?"

"Over there," Deena replied, pointing across the court. "See that man sort of leaning next to the door? Doesn't he look kind of weird?"

"Huh? What man?" Jade demanded.

Deena glanced down. The man had vanished.

A whistle brought their attention back to the game. For the next hour Deena forgot everything but the game.

The Mattewan Blue Sharks were one of Shadyside's main rivals. And the first contest between the two schools was one of the biggest games of the year.

"Go, Tigers!" Jade screamed. Every time Shadyside got the ball, she jumped up in her seat. "Slam it, Teddy!"

Along the sidelines, the cheerleaders did their routines, urging the fans to yell even louder.

At the end of the first half the score was tied at thirty-five. In the second half the lead kept changing. Neither team could get ahead by more than a basket.

"What a game! What a game!" Deena cried. She was on her feet along with everyone else. The cheers were so loud, the bleachers shook, and Deena thought the roof might blow off!

Only a few seconds on the clock. *"De*-fense! *De*-fense!" the Shadyside Tigers cheerleaders cried.

"De-fense!" echoed the fans.

Mattewan called time-out. Deena watched Corky Corcoran, the head cheerleader, do a double flip. Then she led the maroon- and white-uniformed cheerleaders in a loud cheer.

Deena was cheering along when she saw a flash of orange off to one side.

"Hey—!" She leaned forward and peered down the sideline toward the end of the bleachers.

There he was again. The strange man in the orange hunting cap.

He stood on the Shadyside side of the court now. He appeared to be watching the floor, not the game.

Why does he seem so familiar? Deena asked herself.

"Deena!" Jade grabbed her arm. "Deena, what's your problem? The time-out's over!"

Deena focused on the game. The Blue Sharks had a two-point lead. Shadyside had the ball out of bounds with fifteen seconds left.

"Slam it, Teddy!" Jade screamed. "In their face!"

Gary Brandt, the Tigers' captain, dribbled to the basket. He shot. Missed.

It bounced into the hands of a Mattewan guard. The players all began scrambling back toward the Mattewan end of the court.

"Get the ball!" Jade screamed.

Four seconds left.

Deena realized she had been holding her breath, her heart in her throat. "Go, Tigers! Get the ball!" she screamed.

She saw Teddy reach in and steal the ball from the Mattewan guard. He spun back to the basket.

Two seconds. One.

"Shoot!" Jade and Deena screamed in unison. "Shoot!"

Teddy raised the ball and heaved it from center court.

The buzzer rang out.

The ball dropped cleanly through the hoop.

Three points!

Shadyside won!

The bleachers shook as the crowd erupted.

"We won! We won!" Jade hugged Deena.

Deena hugged her back. Over Jade's shoulder, she spotted the man in the orange hunting cap. He was slipping out the door.

Deena still hadn't seen his face. But she had the uncomfortable feeling that she knew him. That she had seen him before.

Why couldn't she remember?

Was he someone she didn't *want* to remember?

They didn't get to Jade's house till late. After the game, Deena and Jade and a bunch of other Shadyside kids piled into Teddy's van and drove to Pete's Pizza to celebrate.

The celebration got more than a little wild. Deena was afraid they'd all be thrown out or arrested for disturbing the peace!

Now she, Jade, and Teddy stood under the pale yellow light over Jade's porch. "Good night, Teddy," Jade said. "Thanks for the ride."

"No problem, Jade," Teddy murmured. He gazed at her as if she were a precious ruby.

Deena turned away and rolled her eyes. Give me a break! she thought.

"See you soon," Jade said. Somehow she managed to make each word about three syllables long.

"I'll call you," Teddy said. He slid his arms around her and they started kissing.

Will you guys hurry it up? Deena uncomfortably. I'm freezing to death!

One of the guys inside the van honked the horn. Then everyone in the van began yelling and whistling.

"Okay, okay!" Teddy cried. He let Jade go and jogged across the walk to the van.

"Teddy's so cool!" Jade gushed, unlocking the front door. "Don't you think he's totally cool?"

"He's okay," Deena said, eager to get inside.

"Just okay? I thought you liked him."

Deena shrugged, then followed Jade upstairs. "Where is everyone?" Deena asked.

"Cathy's staying at a friend's tonight, and Mom went to some hairdressers' party. She'll be home late."

Jade pulled off her jacket and draped it over the doorknob. "Well?" she said, turning to Deena.

"Well, what?" Deena shot back. She dropped her overnight bag on the edge of Jade's bed and sat down to unlace her boots.

"What's your problem?" Jade frowned. "Why are you in such a bad mood? This was an *awesome* night!"

"Yeah. I guess," Deena said reluctantly. "It's just that, well, it seems like you're using Teddy."

Jade laughed, but her smile faded quickly. "What are you talking about, Deena? Sometimes I think you're from Mars!"

"I mean—you don't think Teddy is anyone special," Deena insisted, speaking slowly, thoughtfully.

"He was special tonight!" Jade broke in. "He won the game in the last second!"

"But you don't think he's special the way you think Chuck is," Deena said.

"They're different," Jade replied impatiently. "Teddy's here and Chuck is a hundred miles away at college."

"That's what I'm saying," Deena told her. "You're

just using Teddy. You just want to amuse yourself till Chuck comes back."

"You know what?" Jade flared. "I think you're jealous."

"No!" Deena protested. "It's just that—" She broke off at the sound of tapping.

"Huh? What's that?" she asked.

Jade tilted her head. Both girls stared straight ahead, listening intently.

Silence now. A heavy silence.

Jade shrugged. "Anyway, Deena," she said, frowning, "I don't think that it's your problem if I go out with—"

Tap! Tap! Tap! The sound again. Louder.

"It's coming from the window," Deena whispered, her heart suddenly beating faster. She turned her eyes to the dark curtains over the window.

"It must be the wind," Jade assured her. But her face revealed her fear.

Tap. Tap. Tap. Tap.

"It sounds like someone trying to break in!" Deena said.

"Don't be dumb!" Jade exclaimed. "We're on the second floor."

Tap! Tap! Tap!

"I'm going to call the police!" Deena cried.

"Wait!" Jade insisted. "Maybe it's just a branch."

She clicked off the bedroom light, casting them in darkness.

Deena squinted hard. Watched Jade crawl across

her bed to the window. Jade yanked the curtains apart.

Both girls screamed when they saw the face.

Framed in the window. Pale against the dark sky. The face of a man.

A man in an orange hunting cap, staring in at them.

chapter

4

Deena froze in horror. She couldn't move. She couldn't breathe.

She stared at the cap, struggling to see the man's face. But his features were a dark blur, hidden in shadows.

And then he moved.

Raised his head to the moonlight. Grinned at the frightened girls.

A familiar grin.

"Chuck!" Deena shrieked.

"I'll *kill* him!" Jade cried in a tight, trembling voice. "I'll *kill* him! I really will!" Then she burst out laughing.

"Chuck!" Deena exclaimed. "How did you get up there? What are you *doing?*"

In answer, Chuck tapped on the windowpane again. Deena and Jade worked together to slide the window up.

"Let me in!" Chuck cried. "I'm freezing to death out here!"

The girls reached out and helped pull Chuck in from the large oak branch he was sitting on. He dropped heavily into the room. Then, as he brushed off his jeans, he gave Jade a long, slow, appreciative look.

"You look great," he told her.

"Thanks," she said. "So do you. Nice hat."

Grinning, he pulled off the hat and tossed it onto Jade's bed.

"Chuck—I really don't *believe* you!" Jade exclaimed, hands pressed against her waist. "What are you *doing* here?"

"Later," he replied. He pulled Jade close, giving her a big hug and a kiss.

Then he gave Deena a quick hug. "What's up, Deena?" he asked.

"You're up!" Deena joked. "Up a tree."

"How'd you get up here?" Jade demanded.

"I climbed," Chuck said, shrugging. "Big deal. It was worth it to see the looks on your faces. Man, that was funny!"

"You're about as funny as the stomach flu," Jade told him, shaking her head. But a smile spread across her face.

"When you pulled open the curtains and saw me, I

thought you'd jump out of your skin!" Chuck exclaimed.

"You're a real scary guy, Chuck," Jade replied dryly. "Why didn't you just ring the doorbell like a normal person?"

"Borrr-ring!" Chuck singsonged. "You know I don't like to do things the boring way."

"Tell me about it!" Deena muttered under her breath.

Chuck put on a mock pout. "Aren't you happy to see me?"

"Of course I am," Jade replied. "I'm *very* happy to see you." She took his hand and gave him a smile warm enough to melt an iceberg. "But I thought winter break didn't start till next week."

"It doesn't," Chuck said, and his lopsided grin faded. He turned away. Deena thought she caught a scowl on his face.

"If school's not out, then why are you home?" Deena demanded.

"I had enough of college," Chuck said. "So I decided to start my vacation early."

"Huh? What do you mean, you had enough?" Deena asked.

"I mean I dropped out, okay?" he replied sharply. "There were a couple of professors—they really got on my case."

"Chuck—" Deena started.

"It was all a mistake!" Chuck cried with sudden intense emotion. "The whole thing was a mistake. I never should have gone away to college. It wasn't right for me."

"What's Dad going to say?" Deena asked, crossing her arms over her chest.

"Hey—back off!" Chuck snapped angrily. "Who *cares* what Dad thinks? It's my life." He glared at Deena. "And stop staring at me with that smug, disapproving face. I know what you're thinking, Deena. You're thinking, Poor Chuck. He messed up again. Well, I don't care what you think."

"Fine. Fine," Deena replied, retreating. She hated it when Chuck acted like this. She knew she'd better stop the discussion. She didn't want him to explode.

His expression still menacing, Chuck turned to Jade. "Well? You're not saying anything, Jade. Guess you think I messed up too."

"I—I'm not sure what I think," Jade confessed. "I was just wondering what you're planning to do now."

"I have some ideas," Chuck replied softly.

Deena felt her heart sink. Chuck had obviously gotten into some kind of trouble. Trouble he couldn't bluff his way out of with his easy charm.

She liked Chuck. She loved him. He was her half brother, after all. They shared the same dad. But she had seen this dark side of Chuck before. He was trouble.

He had always been trouble.

Jade dropped onto her bed. "Well?" she asked Chuck. "Are you going to share your ideas with us?"

"Here's what I'm thinking," Chuck replied, sitting

on the bench at Jade's dressing table. "Why was I going to college? To become a filmmaker, right?"

"And you've changed your mind?" Deena asked.

"No. No way," Chuck told her. "But you see, college is all wrong for me. They don't let you just take film courses. You also have to take math, and history, and a lot of other garbage that doesn't have anything to do with making movies."

"Yeah. So?" Jade asked, glancing at Deena, who remained standing in the middle of the bedroom.

"So—why not go where the films are? Why not go to L.A.?" Chuck asked excitedly.

"Really?" squealed Jade.

"Are you crazy?" Deena demanded at the same moment.

"Why not?" Chuck repeated calmly. "I have friends out there. I lived in L.A. with my mom for a while. And that's where the movie business is. Why should I stick around a place like Shadyside, or take dumb classes at a nothing college? Why shouldn't I go where the action is?"

"When are you planning to go?" asked Jade, her eyes wide with excitement.

"As soon as I get some money together," Chuck said.

"I don't believe this!" Deena cried. "Why didn't you tell Mom and Dad you were having trouble in school?"

"Because it's none of their business!" Chuck snapped.

"It's just that I worry about you, Chuck," Deena said.

"Well, stop worrying!" he replied angrily. "Get out of my face, Deena. Stop trying to be my mother, okay? I've already got too many!"

"Stop it, you two!" Jade put her hand on the back of Chuck's neck and began to rub gently. "Now, let's just all calm down. The important thing is that Chuck is here, right?"

"Yeah, yeah," said Chuck sarcastically.

Deena sighed and dropped down on the end of the bed. She watched as Chuck and Jade stared into each other's eyes.

"I'm soooo happy to see you, Chuck," Jade said.

"Yeah. Me too," he told her. "What's up with you, Jade? What have you been up to while I was away?"

"Oh, just the usual. You know—school, hanging out . . ."

"Pretty busy, huh?" Chuck demanded.

"Just the usual," Jade repeated.

"Too busy to write, I mean," he said softly.

"Oh, well, I've never been one for writing letters," Jade said. "You know that, Chuck. But I think about you a lot."

"Yeah," Chuck muttered glumly. "I guess you were thinking about me when you were kissing that other guy tonight."

For a moment the room fell silent.

Oh, wow! Deena thought. Jade is in major trouble now.

But Jade just laughed, her eyes still turned adoringly on Chuck. "You mean Teddy?" she asked innocently.

"Teddy? Who's Teddy?" Chuck demanded.

"He's on the Tigers' team," said Jade. "Deena and I went to the game. Teddy won the game in the last second. And I was just—congratulating him."

"Yeah, sure!" Chuck snarled. He stood up and began pacing the room. "And who else have you been congratulating while I was gone?"

"Chuck!" Jade sounded genuinely hurt. "Give me a break. I've gone out with a few other guys. Of course I have. I mean, I'd die of boredom if I didn't."

She stood up and followed him, putting a hand on his arm. "But I was just killing time. Waiting for you. You've got to believe me."

Jade turned her wide green eyes on him and Deena could practically see Chuck melt. "Do you believe me?" Jade asked softly.

Chuck hesitated. "Yeah. I suppose so."

"Well, good." Jade gave him a quick kiss. "It's so late. Deena and I are totally wrecked from the game. Go on home and we'll get together tomorrow—okay?"

"Okay," Chuck agreed. "The only thing is, I don't exactly feel like facing Dad tonight. Can I have your key, Deena? I'll just let myself in."

"Sure," said Deena. She fished in her bag for her keys and handed them over to Chuck. "But you don't have to worry. Mom and Dad are away. That's why I'm staying at Jade's tonight."

Chuck seemed very relieved. Jade walked Chuck downstairs. From the bedroom, Deena could hear them talking in low voices for several minutes before the front door shut.

Dad is going to have a fit, Deena realized. She dreaded the scene when Chuck spilled the news that he dropped out of school.

Maybe Mom and Dad will get used to the idea, Deena thought hopefully. Maybe they'll even help Chuck get it together to move out to California.

Or maybe there'll be a terrible screaming fight.

"I'm so glad Chuck's back. Aren't you?" Jade asked, strolling back into the bedroom.

"Yes. Of course," Deena replied quickly. But she found herself wondering if she really was glad.

Chuck was always so much trouble. . . .

Deena was still thinking about Chuck when she pulled the covers up to her chin and switched off the light. A few minutes later she managed to forget all about Chuck as she drifted off into a great dream about Steve Mason.

She awoke with a start when the bedroom phone rang. Her eyes popped open and darted around the strange surroundings. It took her a moment to realize she wasn't in her own bedroom.

"Would you get that?" Jade asked groggily. "It's closer to you."

The digital clock showed two-thirty as Deena groped for the receiver. "Hello?" she whispered.

"Hello," rasped a familiar, gravelly voice. Deena jerked up, instantly alert. "Who is this?" she demanded.

"You know," the voice said. "Remember the closet?"

"Who is it?" Jade asked from across the room.

"It's him!" Deena cried.

Jade quickly made her way over to Deena and lowered her head to the phone so she could hear too.

"Remember the closet?" the voice went on. "The one you were hiding in?"

Deena gasped. A year ago she and Jade had hidden in a tiny closet in Farberson's house while he stalked through each room, searching for them. Squashed together, they had huddled, terrified in the back of the dark closet. But Farberson had found them.

No one else knows about the closet, Deena told herself. Jade, me, and Farberson. We're the only ones who know.

That means this caller *has* to be Farberson!

"Go away! Leave us alone!" Deena cried into the phone receiver, her voice tiny and frightened.

"Think about how scared you were that night," the voice whispered. "Because you're going to be *more* scared—real soon."

chapter

5

"*T*hanks, Mrs. Smith," Deena called as Jade's mother dropped her at home on Saturday morning. It was a clear, cold day and Deena squinted into the sun as she walked up the circular driveway to her house.

I wonder if Mom and Dad know that Chuck is home yet, she thought.

As she walked to the back of the house, she heard a door slam and then angry shouting.

They know, all right! Deena thought.

"Why didn't you at least *tell* us you were having problems?" Deena's mom was shouting as Deena opened the back door.

"I didn't think it was any of your business!" Chuck replied heatedly.

Deena stepped into the kitchen. Chuck nodded to her. Her parents ignored her. They were concentrating on Chuck.

It was obvious to Deena that her parents had gone ballistic over Chuck's news. Her mom kept tugging at her hair, pacing back and forth, shaking her head.

Mr. Martinson sat at the kitchen table, gripping his coffee mug so tightly, his knuckles had turned white.

Chuck's face was bright red. He stood in the kitchen doorway, his hands jammed into the front pockets of his jeans, his features set in anger.

"Did you know about this, Deena?" her father demanded.

"Know about what?" Deena tried to sound innocent. She didn't know how much of his plan Chuck had revealed.

"About the trouble Chuck's been in at school," her mother said.

"I'm not in trouble anymore!" Chuck cried breathlessly. "I've already dropped out."

"Deena? *Did* you?" her father demanded.

"The first I knew about anything was last night," Deena told him. She poured herself a glass of orange juice.

"Deena doesn't know anything," Chuck told them with a sneer. "What difference does it make what Deena knows? Dropping out of school was the best thing that could have happened to me."

"Oh, Chuck!" Deena's mom sank into a chair beside the table and lowered her eyes to the floor.

"Well, as long as you're home," Mr. Martinson said, "we're going to set a few things straight. First, you will obey all the family rules—curfew, chores, everything. You will get a job and help with expenses. And—"

"And what else?" Chuck interrupted. "Do I have to wash behind my ears every night?"

"That does it!" Mr. Martinson shouted, slamming his hand down on the table.

"Dear—" cautioned Mrs. Martinson.

"Forget it!" shouted Chuck. "I can see that coming back here was a mistake. You want to run my life! Well, I won't let you! I don't have to listen to you anymore. I'm going to L.A. at the end of the week— and you'll never see me again!"

Chuck was so furious, his entire body was shaking. Deena tried to think of something to say—anything —to calm everyone down.

But Chuck crossed the kitchen and yanked open the back door. He slammed it so hard, the windowpanes rattled. Deena saw him running down the driveway without looking back.

"Is he *crazy?*" Mr. Martinson bellowed. His hands shot out, spilling the coffee mug. "That boy thinks he can get away with anything!" he cried. "This time he's gone too far!"

By late that afternoon, Chuck still hadn't come home. Deena tried calling Jade several times, but her line was always busy.

When she'd finished all her schoolwork, she borrowed her mom's car and drove over to tell Jade what had happened. Maybe Jade will have some idea where Chuck is, Deena thought.

As soon as Jade pulled open her front door, Deena found the answer. Chuck sat on Jade's living-room couch, eating popcorn and watching a video.

Jade was wearing a cat suit as usual. This one made of some kind of shiny yellow material. She had a big gold hoop earring in each ear, and her hair hung in one long braid over her shoulder.

Even on a Saturday afternoon, Jade looks as if she just stepped off the cover of a fashion magazine! Deena marveled to herself.

"Come on in," Jade told Deena with a big smile. "We're watching *Bikini Teen Mutants from Sunset Strip.*"

"I saw it," Deena said. "I thought it was gross."

"Yo, Deena!" Chuck called. He smiled at her as if nothing at all had happened at home. "Check out these zombies."

Deena glanced at the screen. Three teenage girls with pasty white skin and glassy eyes were walking around in tiny bikinis underneath some palm trees.

"Now, *that's* my idea of winter!" Chuck said, grinning and pointing to the screen.

"How do you know it's winter?" Jade asked.

"Doesn't matter. The weather's always warm in L.A. If you don't believe it, then come with me and check it out yourself."

"Yeah. Maybe. Someday," Jade said. "But first I have to finish high school."

"Give me three good reasons why," Chuck challenged. "In fact, give me one good reason."

"What are you guys talking about?" Deena asked, dropping into a green leather armchair.

"Oh, your crazy half brother is trying to convince me to go to L.A. with him," Jade told her, rolling her eyes.

"And Jade's very close to saying yes, aren't you?" Chuck said.

"In your dreams!" Jade replied sharply.

"I'm serious," Chuck insisted. "I can get a job, earn enough money for both of us. If you want to, you can finish school out there."

"Well, maybe someday," Jade repeated. "It's certainly something to think about." Then she flashed Chuck one of her iceberg-melting smiles.

Oh, wow! thought Deena. Can she actually be considering it?

"Well, you have till the end of the week to make up your mind," Chuck told her. "Because no matter what, I'm out of here on Friday."

"Where are you getting the money?" asked Deena.

For a brief flash Deena caught the uncertainty in Chuck's eyes. But then he shrugged and grinned. "I'll get it. No problem."

Deena leaned back against the couch and shut her eyes. Why did Chuck have to hate Shadyside so much?

Why couldn't he just be like other guys and go to college and be normal?

Why did he always have to mess up?

"There's another reason for you to come with me," Chuck said, leaning close to Jade.

"What's that?"

"You'd be safer."

He said it so softly and so seriously that Deena opened her eyes in surprise. "What are you talking about?" she asked.

"I told Chuck about the calls," Jade said.

"Really?" Deena and Jade had decided not to tell anyone.

"Jade says the guy talked about a wrong number, and the closet you two were hiding in," Chuck added.

"Do you think it's Farberson?" Deena demanded, hearing the whispered voice in her mind again.

Chuck shook his head. "No way. Farberson's in jail, right? Maybe it's someone Farberson knows, someone Farberson told the story to."

"Or maybe it's someone who read the details in the newspaper," Jade suggested.

"But it's obviously someone who's really sick," Chuck continued. "Someone who could be dangerous."

Deena felt a little shiver. I should tell Mom and Dad, she thought.

"If you were in California," Chuck told Jade, "you'd be safe from whoever this nut is."

"Chuck, I really don't think—" Jade started to say.

But her words were cut off by the chime of the doorbell. She jumped up and hurried to answer it.

A moment later Jade returned to the living room, holding a stack of envelopes. "Just the mailman," she told them. She began flipping through the envelopes —and abruptly stopped.

She pulled out a long white envelope and tore it open. After removing a folded piece of paper, she smoothed it to read it.

A moment later Jade dropped it with a shriek.

chapter

6

"Jade, what is it?" Deena cried, running to her.

Jade didn't answer. She stared down in horror at the piece of paper, which had fallen onto the coffee table.

As Chuck stepped up behind her, Deena picked up the paper. She studied it—and felt another chill go down her back.

It wasn't a letter. The sheet of typing paper had a drawing pasted on it.

A drawing of a chain saw.

Someone had splattered a red marker on the page to make it look as if blood dripped from the saw. The bright drops of blood led to stark black letters at the bottom of the page: YOUR TURN NEXT.

"I don't believe it!" Jade cried. "This is so gross!"

"Someone is a real sicko," Chuck said softly.

"Well, at least now we know one thing for sure," Deena said, turning her eyes away from the ugly drawing.

"What do we know?" Jade asked.

"We know it couldn't possibly be Farberson," Deena declared. "They censor prison mail—right? The prison would never have let Farberson send this."

"Hey—you're right!" Jade cried. "But, then, who?"

"What if Farberson got out somehow?" Chuck suggested, staring at the chain saw.

Deena swallowed hard. "Th-they wouldn't let him out. He's a murderer," she said softly.

"There's one way to find out," Chuck told her. "Let's drive over to Fear Street to see if anyone is living in Farberson's house."

"Have you totally lost it?" Jade asked him. "The last time we went to Farberson's house, we nearly got killed!"

"We won't get out of the car," Chuck assured her. "We'll just drive past. Check it out. Then drive away as fast as we can. It'll be perfectly safe."

"There won't be anything to see," objected Deena. "I mean, Farberson's house has been deserted since he went to prison. Dad told me so."

"Then there isn't anything to be afraid of," Chuck declared. He stood up. "Come on. Put on your coats. Let's go."

* . * *

47

When they first turned onto Fear Street, it seemed like any other street in Shadyside. But as they drove past Simon Fear's burned-out mansion and the Fear Street cemetery with its ancient tombstones poking up from the ground like skeleton arms, it became easy to see why so many frightening stories were told about the street.

Farberson's house stood on a big lot next to the cemetery.

Deena pulled her mom's Civic up to the crumbling front curb. The fading sunlight made the two-story Victorian house look even creepier than she had remembered it.

"What a wreck!" Deena declared. She could quickly see that nobody had lived in the house for a year. In fact, the house was so run-down, it was as if no one had *ever* lived there!

Several of the windows were boarded up. Others were cracked. The shutters hung loose on their hinges. And the scraggly lawn was overrun with brown weeds poking up through the patches of icy snow.

"Yeah. The house is definitely deserted," Jade murmured.

"Who'd want to move here?" Deena replied. "I mean, after everything that happened?"

"It really looks like a haunted house!" Chuck declared, staring at it. "Think there are ghosts?"

Deena gazed up at the house. "Oh!" She let out a startled cry as a light flickered on in an upstairs window.

A ghostly, flickering light.

"S-someone's in there!" Deena stammered. She stared at the light as if she had been hypnotized.

"Who could it be?" Jade whispered.

"The gas man?" cracked Chuck.

"Chuck, don't be a jerk!" Jade cried. "There's someone in that house. Let's get going! Now!"

"It's just the sun reflecting off the window," Chuck insisted.

"Chuck, the sun is practically down," Deena said. "Let's go!"

She knew that Chuck was just trying to frighten them. It didn't take much to frighten Jade or her in this neighborhood—not after what had happened to them in this house.

"I think we should check it out," Chuck said, reaching for the door handle.

"Chuck!" Jade cried.

"It's probably just some homeless person who's moved in," Chuck said, ignoring Jade's panic.

"Chuck—you promised," Jade said shrilly. "You promised we wouldn't stay. You said—"

But he pushed open the car door and slid out. "Back in a second."

Deena and Jade called to him to come back. But Chuck started jogging across the front yard, up to the front porch.

"I don't *believe* him!" Deena cried. "He's crazy. He's just *crazy!* He promised—"

"Deena—look!" Jade shrieked. She pointed to the house.

Deena raised her eyes to the upstairs window. To her surprise, the pale light had moved.

The house lay in darkness. Then, as she stared up at the house, she saw the light flicker in a downstairs window.

"Whoever has the light—came downstairs!" Jade whispered.

"We've got to warn Chuck!" Deena cried.

Where *was* Chuck?

Deena squinted into the hazy twilight. "Oh, no!" she shouted.

Chuck had climbed onto the front porch. Did he plan to go in?

Deena and Jade shoved open their car doors and screamed a desperate warning. "Chuck! Chuck! Don't go in!"

chapter

7

"Oh, no!" Jade shrieked. "He's going in! I've got to get him!"

"Jade, no—!" Deena pleaded. But her friend had already climbed out of the car and was running up the lawn toward the porch. She slipped once on a patch of icy snow, but kept on going, calling Chuck's name.

Chuck turned around and said something Deena couldn't hear.

Jade pointed upstairs and said something back. They seemed to be arguing.

Hurry up, you two, Deena urged silently. We've got to get out of here!

And then she saw something else, something Chuck and Jade couldn't see.

Another light.

A light flickering from *behind* the house.

And then Deena heard the grind and cough of an engine starting up.

She turned her head and searched the empty street.

No. The sound didn't come from the street.

It came from behind the house.

"Jade! Chuck!" she yelled. "Someone's coming!"

Jade and Chuck stopped arguing and turned toward the street. They must have heard the engine too, Deena realized.

She saw Chuck leap off the porch and start toward the back of the house. Jade grabbed his hand and began pulling him in the opposite direction.

"Come back! Hurry!" Deena shouted frantically. Her heart pounding, she dived back into the car. After sliding behind the wheel, she turned the key and revved the engine.

Deena stared out at Jade and Chuck. Jade won the argument, Deena decided. She watched the two of them jog to the car.

The engine behind the house roared louder.

Jade and Chuck were halfway across the yard, when Jade slipped again. This time she fell into the snow.

Chuck bent over her.

"My ankle, my ankle!" Deena hear Jade cry.

"Hurry! *Please!* Hurry!" Deena screamed.

The light behind the house had faded. The yard was bathed in a blue-gray darkness now.

Deena watched Chuck tenderly put his arm around

52

Jade's waist. She seemed to be having trouble getting to her feet in the snow.

Hurry, hurry, hurry. Deena repeated her silent plea.

The engine roar faded. Changed. No longer the sound of an engine revving up.

Now it became the steady hum of a moving car—a car rolling down the driveway.

"Chuck! Jade!" Deena's voice came out choked and frightened.

Chuck still had his arm around Jade's waist. Jade took a hobbling step—and then froze, staring at the side of the house.

As Deena squinted into the darkness, a car came bouncing out from behind the house.

Its headlights had been off, Deena realized.

It wheeled off the driveway. Onto the front lawn.

Picking up speed.

Faster. Faster.

Straight at Chuck and Jade.

chapter

8

Deena called frantically to her friends. But they were frozen in place.

The car picked up speed as it roared across the snow-patched lawn.

The driver is trying to run them down! Deena realized. "Run! Come on—run!" she shrieked.

Finally Jade and Chuck started to move. They lurched toward the street, Jade stumbling and sliding as Chuck tried to help her.

Deena leaned over and popped open the passenger door. The dark car moved closer, bouncing the whole way.

Jade dove into the backseat. Chuck slid in beside

Deena, breathing hard. "Go! Go! Go!" he screamed breathlessly.

The car doors still open, Deena floored the gas pedal. The car jerked away from the curb, tires squealing.

In the rearview mirror Deena saw the other car bounce off the curb, spin into the street.

It tried to ram right into us! she realized.

"Go! Go! Go!" Chuck repeated. He twisted in the seat to peer out the back window. "It—it's chasing us!"

Deena saw the headlights flash on. White light swept into the car.

"Go! Go! Go!"

"I can't go any faster!" Deena shrieked, and roared through a stop sign. The tires skidded over an icy patch. The car jolted forward, slid, then shot ahead.

"It—it's catching up!" Jade wailed from the back-seat. "What are we going to do?"

Deena couldn't answer. She was concentrating too hard to think. The dark trees and front yards of Fear Street whirred past as if in a dream. The only light came from the bouncing headlights of the car chasing them.

Deena reached Old Mill Road, flew around the corner without looking, wrestling the car to stay on the road. The tires squealed in protest. A horn blared. Brakes screeched.

Faster. Down the dark, empty street.

The other car turned too. The invading light swept through the car.

"It—it's right behind us!" Jade uttered in a tight, frightened voice. "It—"

They bounced as the car bumped them hard from behind.

"Ohh!" Deena screamed, and her hands slipped off the wheel.

Deena's car lurched to the left. Another horn blared. She saw the blur of a red van swerving out of her way.

Another hard bump.

"He's trying to bump us off the road!" Chuck cried.

"I can't go any faster!" Deena shouted, leaning over the wheel, squinting ahead. The little Civic shook as Deena pumped the gas pedal.

Another hard bump from behind.

And then the other car pulled left. Shot forward. Came up beside them.

Deena turned her eyes from the road. Could she see the other driver?

A blaring horn.

An oncoming pickup.

But Deena and the other car were side by side. Blocking the whole street.

We're going to hit head-on! Deena realized.

Head-on. Head-on. Head-on.

She stomped on the brake.

Too late.

A deafening squeal. A long skid.

The crunch of metal. The high tinkle of shattering glass.

Then everything went dark.

chapter

9

*J*ade's high-pitched scream filled the car.

Deena swallowed hard, fighting back the tremors of fear that shook her body.

We're still moving, she realized.

We're still speeding through the darkness.

The darkness.

Why had everything suddenly gone dark? Because the other two cars had collided. Their headlights no longer sweeping over Deena's car.

She raised her eyes to the rearview mirror.

Saw the car and truck nose to nose. Saw the drivers stepping out.

They're okay, Deena realized.

And we're okay. We're not hit. We're moving. Moving toward home.

We got away.
This time.

They settled into Jade's living room. The house felt warm and comforting. Jade's parents had gone to bed.

Jade made mugs of steaming hot chocolate. Deena sank into a soft armchair and let out a long sigh of relief. She could still feel the bumping of the car, still hear the crash of metal and glass.

"Who was he?" Chuck asked, shaking his head. "Why did he try to kill us?"

"It wasn't a he," Deena revealed, holding the white mug in her lap, letting it warm both hands.

"Huh?" Jade and Chuck uttered in unison.

"It was a woman," Deena told them. "I saw her. She had long hair."

"We have to call the police," Jade said softly, very pale, her expression still tight with fear.

"We can't," Chuck replied quickly. "They'll ask us what we were doing back at that house. They'll accuse us of—of looking for trouble."

"Then we have to tell our parents," Deena insisted.

"No way!" Chuck replied firmly. "They'll ask the same questions. They'll ground you and Jade forever. I'm out of here next week. But you two will be in major trouble."

Deena caught the thoughtful expression on Jade's face. "I think I know who it was," Jade said. "Tell me again what the driver of the car looked like."

"I saw her for only a second," Deena said. "She had

blondish hair, a pale face. But maybe that was just from the headlights."

"Then I know who it was," Jade replied. "And I'm positive it's the same person who's making the frightening calls."

"You're kidding!" Deena lowered the white mug to the coffee table. "How could you possibly know that?"

"Think about it," Jade said, tossing back her hair. "Who is the one person who knows what happened last year—and had a key to the Farberson house?"

"Farberson's girlfriend!" Deena exclaimed.

"Right!" Jade said.

"But it's a year later. Why was she at the house?" Deena demanded. "And why would she come barreling over the front lawn to try to chase us off?"

"I don't know," Jade admitted. Then her eyes narrowed as she added, "Don't you think we ought to ask her?"

"Whoa! Wait a minute!" Deena went on. "It couldn't be her. The person who made the calls is a man, or have you forgotten that?"

"Anyone can disguise her voice," Jade reasoned. "In fact, I read about a little electronic gadget that can make a man sound like a woman or a woman sound like a man."

"But why would Farberson's girlfriend call us? Why would she do any of those things?"

"Only one way to find out," Jade replied. She opened the drawer in the oak table beside the couch and pulled out the Shadyside phone book. "Now, what was her name?"

Deena shut her eyes and thought. "Linda? Linda something, right?"

"Morrison!" Jade added. "Linda Morrison. I remember now from the restaurant." She opened the phone book to the *M*'s and ran her finger down the column. "L. M. Morrison. On Pike Street. That's her. I recognize the address."

"You mean you're just going to call her?" Deena gasped.

"No. I thought it would be better to visit her, and ask in person," Jade replied, raising her eyes from the phone book.

"Are you crazy?" cried Deena. "She just tried to run us off the road!"

"If we go to her house, it will show her we're not afraid of her," Jade replied. "She'll know we know what she's doing. And she'll have to stop."

Deena swallowed hard. "When do you want to visit her?"

Jade slammed the phone book shut. "How about tomorrow?"

chapter
10

*T*he next morning Deena awoke to the sound of shouting from downstairs. For a moment she thought she was still dreaming. But then she remembered everything that had happened the day before.

Oh, no, she thought, burying her head under the pillow. Chuck and my parents are at it again.

Couldn't Chuck *try* to get along with them for five minutes?

Maybe I should stay in bed all day, she thought. But she pulled herself up, washed, and brushed her teeth, then slipped into her robe.

The shouting grew louder as Deena made her way down the stairs.

"As long as you're living here, you'll follow the house rules!" she heard her father scream.

"Just get out of my face! Stop trying to run my life!" Chuck screamed back.

Deena heard a loud pounding sound. Then Chuck shouted again. "Awww, forget it!" Once again the kitchen door slammed so hard that the entire house shook.

When Deena entered the kitchen, both her parents were staring at the kitchen door. Through the window she could see Chuck disappearing around the side of the house.

"Good morning," Deena said in a small voice.

"Oh, good morning, dear," said her mother, chewing her bottom lip.

"More trouble with Chuck, huh? Where'd he go?" Deena asked.

"Who knows?" grumbled her father. "Who cares?" Scowling, he sat at the table and picked up the Sunday paper.

Mrs. Martinson gave him a worried glance, then turned back to the stove. "I'm making blueberry pancakes this morning," she told Deena. "How many do you want?"

Deena was starting on her second stack, when she heard a knock at the back door. Jade hurried in without waiting for anyone to open it.

She was wearing a powder-blue wool skirt and turtleneck under a navy jacket, with stockings and navy pumps. Deena had never seen her dressed that way before.

"Good morning, Jade," said Mrs. Martinson. "Don't you look nice! So grown-up!"

"Thanks," Jade replied, beaming. "Hi, Deena. Ready to go that party with me?"

"Party?" Deena asked, not understanding.

"You know," Jade said, flashing her a meaningful glance. "That business party my mom is giving that I said we'd help her with?"

"Oh, *that* party!" Deena exclaimed, catching on. "I totally forgot."

"That's obvious," said Jade, motioning to Deena's bathrobe.

"Can I help Jade with her mom's party?" Deena asked her mother.

"I suppose so," Mrs. Martinson replied. "Have you finished all your homework?"

"Most of it," Deena replied. She jumped up, leaving the pancakes, and hurried up to her room. "What's up?" she asked Jade, closing her bedroom door.

"I've figured out how we can find out what's going on with Linda Morrison," Jade announced in a whisper.

"Oh, no!" protested Deena. "Jade, I'm not—"

"Relax!" Jade instructed. "I'll explain it all on the way. Just change your clothes. What do you have that looks really businessy?"

Deena stared into her open closet, then pulled out a maroon A-line dress that her mother had bought her the year before. Deena never wore it because it made her look too much like her mother. "How's this?" she asked.

"Perfect," Jade replied. "We'll just dress it up with a scarf."

While Deena pulled on the dress, Jade began rummaging through Deena's dresser. She pulled out a black- and gold-striped scarf and knotted it at Deena's throat.

"Come on," she said. "I've got my mom's car only till one."

A few moments later Deena slid in beside Jade in the front seat of the Chevy. "Now will you tell me what's going on?"

"Here's the deal," said Jade. "I figured out a way we can ask questions and snoop around without Linda Morrison suspecting anything. I borrowed some wigs from my mom's beauty shop so Linda won't recognize us."

"But how are we going to get into her house?"

"I already took care of that," Jade replied, her eyes lighting up excitedly. "First, I drove by her house this morning. Guess what I saw? A big FOR SALE BY OWNER sign in front."

"Yeah. So what?" Deena demanded. She always had trouble following these schemes of Jade's.

"So I went home and called her," Jade continued impatiently. "I told her I'm a real estate agent, and that I've sold a lot of homes in her area. I told her I was sure I could find a buyer."

"And she believed you?"

"What do *you* think?" Jade replied. "I know how real estate people talk. My aunt has been selling houses for years. Anyway, I told her 'my associate' and I would be over later this morning to examine her property."

Deena remained silent for a moment. "Jade—even with wigs and these dreadful clothes, Linda Morrison is going to recognize us."

"She hasn't seen us in a year," Jade argued. "Besides, when I get through making us up, our own mothers won't know us!"

"I hope you're right."

"I know I am. Anyway, the important thing is to get in there and find out what's going on."

She pulled the car into a gas station and parked by the curb. "Come on," she urged, pulling a big shopping bag out of the backseat.

Deena followed Jade into the ladies' room. Jade had a shoulder-length auburn wig for Deena and a cap of curly black hair for herself. She pulled out a makeup kit and got to work.

A few minutes later Deena stared at a stranger in the mirror. "Wow!" she declared, admiring herself. "I look at least twenty years old!"

"I told you," Jade replied. "There's no way Linda Morrison will remember who we are."

Deena turned to Jade's reflection. Jade looked glamorous with the dark curly hair and her sparkling green eyes and creamy-white, perfect skin. She turned around once in front of the mirror, then folded up the bags.

"Remember," Jade instructed as they walked back to the car. "Keep your eyes and ears open. And let me do most of the talking."

The one-story wooden house was small. It sat on a tiny lot, squeezed between two other similar houses.

As they stood on the front porch, Deena felt her heart begin to pound. She swallowed hard, her mouth dry.

What if Jade were wrong? What if Linda Morrison *did* recognize them?

She had tried to run them down last night.

What would she do if she had Jade and Deena trapped in her house?

I've changed my mind, Deena thought. I want to get out of here.

Jade always has the craziest plans. Why do I always go along with them? Why do I always get suckered in?

This was a major mistake. I want to leave—fast.

But before she could tell Jade, the front door opened. Linda Morrison peered out at them.

She's gained a lot of weight since the last time we saw her, Deena realized. Morrison's blond hair had dark roots now and was pulled back into a ponytail. Her face seemed puffy, older.

"Yes?" she asked, her voice flat and unfriendly.

"Miss Morrison?" Jade began in a businesslike voice. "I'm Louise Smith and this is my associate,

Darlene Mathers. I called this morning about representing your property?"

"Oh, yeah. Right," Morrison replied. "Come on in."

Deena held back for a second, her heart pounding. Then she followed Jade into the house.

The small living room smelled of bacon. Deena could see the remains of breakfast on a small table against the far wall.

Papers and magazines were piled on every surface. Deena could see a thick layer of dust on the windowsills. Not much of a housekeeper, Deena thought.

"Just push some of that stuff on the floor and sit down," Morrison instructed. "I haven't had a chance to straighten up lately."

"This is a good-size room," Jade commented, studying the cluttered living room. "We can get someone to come in and clean up."

"Whatever," Morrison replied with a shrug.

Jade pulled out a notebook and pen. "Now, I'll need some information from you before I can list the property," she said. "First of all, how long have you had the for-sale sign up?"

"A couple of days," the woman replied. "But you're the first person who's noticed it."

"It's been my experience that sales by the owner don't attract very many buyers," Jade said smoothly. "By dealing with my agency, you'll reach a lot more people. I'll place advertising, have an open house . . ."

"Unh-unh." Morrison shook her head. "I don't want a lot of strangers coming through here."

"Fine," Jade replied quickly, making a note on her pad. "We'll show it by appointment only, then."

Deena gazed at Jade. Where did her friend learn all these real-estate terms? She sounded so professional, Deena started to relax.

"When are you planning to move out?" Jade continued.

"As soon as possible," Linda Morrison answered. "Tomorrow, if I could."

"I see," said Jade. "And can you tell me why you're in such a hurry?"

"What business is that of yours?" Morrison snapped. She narrowed her eyes at Jade.

"Uh—just wondering," Jade said smoothly. "In case I would need to reach you out of town."

"Is that right?" Morrison said. "By the way, you haven't showed me your business card yet."

"My business card?" Jade's confident expression faded. "Are you sure I didn't give it to you?"

"Positive," Linda Morrison answered sharply, holding out her hand. "I really must insist on seeing it."

Oh, wow, Deena thought, her heart sinking to her knees. We're dead!

chapter

11

Linda Morrison crossed her arms over her chest. "I'm waiting," she said coldly.

"No problem," Jade replied. She opened her purse and began to rummage through it. "It's here somewhere," she murmured.

Now what? Deena asked herself.

What do we do? Jade can't stall her forever, pretending to look for a business card.

She turned her eyes to the front door. Should we just make a run for it?

When Deena glanced back, she found Jade smiling. "Here it is," she declared. She pulled a small white card from the bag and handed it to Linda Morrison.

Morrison held it close, staring at it suspiciously. "Louise Smith, Real Estate," she read. "Okay."

Deena gaped at the card and then at her friend. Where had Jade found the business card?

Jade reached out for the card, but Linda held on to it. "Now, my associate and I will need to take some measurements in here before we can list the house. Don't let us disturb you," Jade said with a smile.

"Go ahead," Linda Morrison told her. "I've got some things to do in the back of the house anyway."

"Come on, Darlene," said Jade.

Deena sat there, still dazed, waiting for her heart to stop thundering.

"I said, come on, *Darlene!*" Jade repeated.

"Oh, right," Deena said, forcing herself to snap out of it.

Jade pulled out a metal tape measure and began to measure the walls. Linda Morrison disappeared into the back.

As soon as she was gone, Deena grabbed her friend's wrist. "Where did you get that business card?" she whispered.

"It's my aunt's," Jade explained. "No problem." She glanced toward the hallway. "We don't have much time," she whispered. "There's got to be something here that will help us. Why don't you check in that pile of stuff on the table. I'll go through the desk."

Feeling like a burglar, Deena began to sort through a stack of papers on the edge of the coffee table. There were old phone bills, supermarket coupons, advertisements for takeout pizza, and half-finished crossword puzzles. Nothing to explain why Linda Morrison could have been at the Farberson house the night before.

At the bottom of the pile she found a notepad filled with doodles and diagrams. Deena was flipping through the pages, when she heard Jade gasp.

"I've found something!" Jade whispered excitedly.

"Huh? What?"

"Look at this! From the bottom desk drawer." Jade held up a key chain. "Two house keys!" she announced. "And the keychain is labeled Farberson! What do you have there?" Jade asked, gazing at the notepad in Deena's hand.

"Just some drawings," said Deena. "I don't know what they—"

"That's Farberson's house!" Jade cried. "Look at the address!"

Deena lowered her eyes to the bottom of the page. To her surprise, Jade was right—884 Fear Street. She was holding a crude diagram of Farberson's house.

The downstairs was drawn in one square. It showed the kitchen and dining room and living room. The living room where they had found Mrs. Farberson's body a year ago.

The upstairs was drawn in a second square. It showed four bedrooms. Deena recognized the bedroom where they had hidden in the tiny closet on that terrifying night.

"Why do you suppose she has this?" Deena whispered.

"I don't know," Jade replied with a shrug. "But it's

proof! Proof that she's still interested in the Farberson house—and proof that she could have been the one who chased us!"

"Not enough proof," Deena replied. "I'd like to take a look at her car."

"Good idea," Jade whispered. "I'll ask her if we can get into the garage, and then—" Her words were cut off by a door banging open.

Her heart pounding in alarm, Deena turned to the hall.

"All right, girls," Linda Morrison snapped. She stood in the doorway. "That's enough. I remember who you two are. So why don't we just cut to the chase!"

chapter

12

Deena gasped in shock.

But Jade recovered quickly. "Excuse me?" she replied.

"You heard me," Linda Morrison said softly, her eyes narrowed at Jade. "I said I remember who you are. What are you doing here in my house?"

"I'm Louise Smith," Jade insisted. "And this is—"

But Deena could see the woman wasn't buying Jade's lies. "Drop it," Linda Morrison snapped, holding the business card Jade had given her. "I just called the real-estate office and they said Louise Smith is on vacation. You're the two girls who messed in Stanley's problems last year. Now, what are you doing here? Why are you snooping around?"

Deena's legs began to tremble. She could feel every muscle in her body tightening in fear.

But Jade coolly gazed back at the woman. "I might ask you a few questions," Jade said. "For example, why have you been making those phone calls to us?"

"Phone calls?" Morrison acted confused. "What are you talking about?"

"Don't pretend you don't know about them," Jade replied sharply. "Why did you try to run us over last night?"

"Run you over?" Morrison asked. "Then that was you last night?"

"You knew who it was!" Jade accused. "What's going on?"

Deena stared at her friend in admiration. The Morrison woman had caught them lying, but Jade had turned it around and put Morrison on the spot.

"I'm sorry. I was only trying to find out who you were," the woman said, her voice shaking.

"Do you expect us to believe that?" Jade demanded.

"It's the truth!" Morrison insisted. "When I saw your car out by the curb, I got scared to death."

"If you were so scared," Deena demanded, "why did you deliberately try to run down Jade and Chuck?"

"I couldn't see anything," Morrison explained. "I was using a borrowed car, and I couldn't figure out how to turn on the headlights."

Yeah, right! Deena thought sarcastically. That's why she rammed our car three times. She must think we're morons. Who'd believe that story?

But to Deena's surprise, the woman's expression changed. Her features crumpled and tears appeared in her pale blue eyes.

"I'm really sorry," she sniffled. "I wasn't trying to hurt anyone—or even scare you. I was just trying to protect myself."

"From what?" Jade asked, exasperated. "And how could making scary phone calls to us protect you?"

"I—I didn't make any calls," Morrison insisted. She dabbed at her eyes with a tissue. "I'm sorry if you were scared. But you don't know how I've felt. I've been so—stressed out, so frightened, for months."

"Why?" asked Jade.

"It's *him,*" Morrison replied heatedly. "Stanley. I know he's in prison. But I'm terrified that he'll get out and come after me. He blamed me for everything!"

"How could he get out?" Deena cried, finally finding her voice. "He was sentenced to life, right?"

"Stanley is much more clever than you can imagine," Morrison sobbed. "He and his lawyer have been working on an appeal. Something to do with a legal mistake. If he wins his appeal, he could be out this month."

"No!" Deena gasped. "There must be some mistake, Ms. Morrison!"

"Call me Linda," the older woman said. She shook

her head. "I'm so sorry to break the news to you, girls. I know you must find it frightening too."

"But he killed his wife!" Deena cried. "I can't believe they'd just let him go free."

"It happens all the time," Linda replied bitterly. "If Stanley can prove that the police didn't follow the law perfectly, he can get out."

"The month is almost over," Deena said thoughtfully. "Could he be out already?"

If Farberson is out, it would explain the nasty phone calls, Deena thought. And the drawing of the chain saw. It would explain everything.

"No, he's not out yet," Linda assured them. "My lawyer promised to let me know when it happens. Besides, the minute he's free, Stanley will come after me. I know he will."

"I'm still confused about something," Jade said. "What were you doing at his house on Fear Street last night?"

For a moment the older woman didn't answer. "I suppose I might as well tell you," she said finally. "You know that Stanley stole a lot of money from his restaurant. Before he murdered his wife."

"Yes, we remember," Jade said.

"Well, before Stanley was arrested, he told me he hid it somewhere in the house. He wanted me to put it somewhere safe."

"So what did you do?" Jade demanded.

"I tried to find it," Linda replied. "But I couldn't."

She sighed. "Stanley didn't believe me. He accused me of stealing it. He phoned me from prison a few weeks ago. He said that if I don't come up with the money by the time he gets out, he'll kill me!"

"So you've been searching the house for the money?" Deena guessed.

"I've looked everywhere," Linda replied, her eyes again brimming with tears. "That's all I've been doing for weeks. But I can't find it. And I think I know why."

"Why?" Jade asked.

"Someone else must have taken it," Linda said. "Someone else who knew it was there."

Her expression changed. She glared at Jade, then at Deena. "I just figured it out!" Linda Morrison exclaimed. "Oh, man. I've been so stupid. But I just figured it out. *You* took the money—didn't you?"

The woman moved quickly to block the front doorway. "I'm right—aren't I!" she cried, studying them both. *"You* took the money!"

Deena was about to protest. But Jade, as usual, spoke first. "Yes, you're right. We took it all," Jade confessed.

chapter

13

Deena gasped. What was Jade saying? Had she lost her mind?

"We took the money," Jade repeated. "Then we flapped our arms and flew to the moon."

Linda Morrison stared hard at Jade. "What are you saying?"

"I'm saying that's crazy," Jade told her. "Deena and I didn't know about any hidden money."

"That's a good story," Linda replied sharply. "But I know different. I know that the night Stanley caught you last year, you were searching his house. What else could you have been looking for?"

"We were looking for papers," Jade replied. "Looking for some kind of proof that Farberson was guilty.

Deena's brother Chuck had been accused. We were trying to find something that would prove Chuck was innocent."

Morrison studied them. "Why should I believe you?" she demanded. "All I know is, the money is gone. And Stanley will blame me."

"Well, we didn't know about it. And we didn't take it!" Jade insisted.

Linda blew her nose and sighed. And now her mood seemed to change again. "I suppose I have no choice but to believe you," she said.

"Maybe Farberson lied about hiding the money," Deena offered.

"I thought of that," Linda told her. "But if so, why is he threatening me? In any case, I give up. I'm not looking for it anymore. Last night was my last attempt."

"What are you going to tell Farberson?" Jade asked.

"Nothing," said Linda. "I'm too afraid to even think about talking to him again. I've decided to move someplace far from here, where he can never find me. That's why my house is up for sale. As a matter of fact, I was starting to pack when you called this morning."

"Well, good luck," Deena said, not knowing what else to say.

"Thanks," Linda replied. "And good luck to you girls too." She narrowed her eyes at them. "If Stanley gets out, you may need it."

* * *

Deena spent the rest of the afternoon working on her algebra and a history paper. She kept listening for Chuck to come home. But there was no sign of him.

Jade called at six. Her mom and sister had gone to visit Jade's aunt. She invited Deena over for pizza.

"Thanks for getting me out of the house," Deena said when Jade opened the door. "It's a nightmare there. My parents are so mad at Chuck."

"Good thing he's over here, then," Jade said, gesturing toward the sofa.

"Chuck!" cried Deena. "Do Mom and Dad know you're here?"

Chuck gave her a sour scowl that told her he was sick of talking about the whole situation. "As far as I'm concerned," he said, "they don't need to know anything about me—ever."

Deena decided to keep her mouth shut. She sat down on one of the armchairs across from Chuck. From the two pizza crusts on a paper plate, she could see that he already had a head start on dinner.

"Have a root beer," Jade offered, handing Deena a glass.

"So Jade was just telling me about your big adventure this afternoon," Chuck said, pulling another slice from the carton.

Deena snickered. "You should have seen Jade with short, curly black hair."

81

"I'll bet she looked great!" Chuck gushed, gazing at Jade admiringly.

"I told him what Linda said about the money," Jade said. "I told him she thinks the money isn't there anymore. But Chuck says—"

"I think the woman is lying," Chuck interrupted.

"Why would she lie?" Deena asked.

"Because she doesn't want anyone else to get it," Chuck replied impatiently. "The Morrison woman may be going away, but I'll bet she still wants to get her hands on the money."

"Chuck could be right," Jade said thoughtfully. "Think about it. Remember how she kept saying over and over that the money was gone?"

"That's because it *is* gone!" Deena exclaimed.

"No, it's because she didn't want *us* to find it!" Jade declared.

"She told you about the money to see if you girls knew anything about it," Chuck explained. "Then, when she found out you didn't, she wanted you to think it wasn't in the house after all."

"Well, maybe you're right," Deena agreed. "But so what?"

"So—I think that money is ours!" Chuck exclaimed, grinning.

"Chuck!" Deena gasped. "You don't mean—"

"I don't know how much there is," he continued, ignoring her. "But it will go a long way toward getting me to Los Angeles."

"You can't take that money!" Deena protested.

"Why not?" Chuck replied, still grinning. "We deserve it after everything we went through last year. In a way, you could say we *earned* it!"

"Jade, talk him out of it!" Deena pleaded.

"I think I agree with Chuck," Jade confessed. "I mean, it's not like we're robbing a bank or anything. The money is already there—and no one knows it's there. And we did go through a lot because of Farberson. I mean, Chuck ended up in jail, and you and I nearly got killed!"

"But it's illegal money!" Deena protested. "Farberson stole it."

"The insurance company has probably paid everyone by now," Chuck said, finishing his third slice and dropping the crust onto his paper plate. "Don't be such a wimp, Deena. It's free money. And it can be ours!"

For a moment Deena just stared at her brother. How could Chuck even be thinking of trying to find that money?

Jade is nearly as bad, Deena decided. How could she encourage him?

"So what do you say?" Chuck asked, jumping up. "How about a little treasure hunt?"

"You mean tonight?" Jade cried, surprised.

"The sooner the better," Chuck told them.

"I don't know if I'm ready to go back there," Jade said, biting her lower lip. "Especially after last night."

"Let's go to a movie or something instead," Deena suggested.

Ignoring them, Chuck made his way to the front entryway.

"Chuck—come back!" Jade called. "We have to talk about this some more."

"I don't need your permission," Chuck called back. "I don't even need your help." He pulled open the front door.

"Chuck, no!" Deena pleaded.

"Last chance to come with me!" Chuck announced. He stepped out into the dark.

Deena and Jade followed him onto the porch. "Jade, you've got to stop him!" Deena pleaded.

"I'm trying!" Jade said. She ran down the sidewalk after Chuck, screaming his name over and over. "Chuck, please stop! Listen to me! Chuck!"

Jade grabbed his shirt and he struggled, pushing her aside. "No! Don't!" she wailed.

Deena started after them. But she stopped when she saw someone standing under the streetlight at the curb.

His face was buried in shadows.

But Deena could see that he was tall. And broad.

Dressed in black.

Farberson?

She opened her mouth to call to Jade and Chuck.

Too late.

The man burst out from behind the light post.

He grabbed Chuck. They wrestled for a moment.

Jade uttered a frightened scream as the man wrapped Chuck in a choke hold.

Deena watched Chuck sink to his knees, his arms flailing wildly, helplessly, as the man, grunting and cursing, strangled him.

chapter

14

In the pale, hazy light from the street lamp, the scene in front of her seemed like a dream to Deena.

Chuck lay sprawled on his back at the foot of the driveway, the big man pressing him down. Jade shrieking as she tried frantically to pull the man off Chuck.

A terrifying dream.

And as Deena ran down the driveway, she entered the dream.

Jade's frightened cries grew louder.

The intruder's grunts and groans rose on the still night air.

Chuck didn't move.

"Chuck! Chuck!" Deena repeated his name as she ran.

And then another name burst into her ears.

"Teddy—stop! Teddy!"

Jade's desperate cries. "Teddy—please!"

And Deena realized the powerful intruder wasn't a stranger. She recognized Teddy. The basketball game flashed into her mind. Teddy's heroic shot at the sound of the buzzer.

Teddy had seemed so light on the basketball floor. So graceful and light.

And now he had become a heavy monster, strangling Deena's brother, leaning on Chuck's still body, holding him down.

"Let me up!" Chuck pleaded weakly.

Not dead. Not strangled!

Deena breathed a long sigh, her heart still thudding.

"Let go of him! Teddy—let go!" Jade's shrill pleas.

A neighbor's lights flashed on. And the lights flickered on in the house across the street.

Slowly, breathing hard, Teddy backed away.

"Teddy—why?" Jade cried shrilly, tugging him away. "Why?"

"I heard you screaming at him," Teddy replied, breathing hard. "I saw you running after him, yelling at him. I saw him push you. I thought he was hurting you—"

"But he's Deena's brother!" Jade cried.

But before Teddy could say anything, Chuck startled them all by jumping to his feet.

"Chuck—no!" Deena screamed.

Too late.

With a loud groan, Chuck pulled back his arm—and swung his fist hard at Teddy.

The punch went wild as Teddy ducked. Chuck staggered forward, off balance. Teddy landed a hard punch on Chuck's shoulder.

"Stop it, you two! Stop it!" Jade shrieked.

Deena covered her eyes. Why won't they stop? Why are they doing this?

She opened her eyes in time to see Teddy land a solid punch on Chuck's face. Chuck's nose began to bleed, bright red blood streaming down his face onto his sweatshirt.

Chuck staggered, his eyes wild with surprise. Deena thought he would go down. But then he came back at Teddy with a shout—and began beating frantically on the bigger boy's back and sides.

Teddy grunted with pain, then twisted around and pulled himself away from Chuck.

Chuck's face twisted with fury. He ran toward Teddy again, the full weight of his body behind him.

Teddy dived to one side.

Chuck staggered forward. Stumbled.

Fell.

Deena heard the crack as his head hit the curb. The sound seemed to split the air. It forced Deena to shut her eyes again.

"Chuck!" Jade was shrieking. "Chuck!"

Chuck didn't answer.

Deena opened her eyes.

Chuck lay sprawled facedown in a dark pool of blood.

His head twisted to the side at an odd angle. The one eye Deena could see was open wide, staring blankly down the street.

Deena dived to her knees beside him. "He's unconscious!" she wailed.

Teddy pushed in beside her. "Don't move him!" he warned breathlessly. Sweat dripped down his forehead. He placed a hand on the side of Chuck's neck. "Good—I can feel his pulse."

Hearing voices, Deena glanced over her shoulder. A crowd of neighbors had gathered on the curb. Turning back to Chuck, Deena could hear their murmured questions behind her:

"What happened?"

"Who is he?"

"What's going on? Were they fighting?"

"Did anyone call an ambulance?" Jade was screaming. "Did anyone call 911?"

Please, Deena thought, staring at her brother. Please let Chuck be all right.

Chuck stirred but didn't awaken.

Deena heard the shrill wail of sirens.

The street soon pulsed with flashing red and blue lights. Police arrived first. Then the white-suited medics.

A young police officer ushered Deena, Jade, and

Teddy to the side. Deena struggled to concentrate on the woman's questions. She kept glancing over her shoulder to see what the medics were doing to Chuck.

He'll be okay, Deena told herself. He'll be okay.

But he's in trouble once again.

Poor Chuck. Always in trouble.

"He's my brother," Deena heard herself telling the officer. "Chuck Martinson."

"How was he hurt?" the officer demanded.

Jade answered immediately. "It was an accident," she said. "The two boys were messing around. Chuck fell."

Deena relaxed. As usual, Jade knew what to do to keep Chuck from getting in even more trouble.

"Is that so?" the officer asked, squinting at Jade. "The neighbors reported a fight."

Again Jade answered smoothly. "That's probably what it looked like," she said. "But the guys were just goofing. They're really good friends, right, Teddy?"

"Right," Teddy mumbled.

The police cars rolled away, their lights still flashing. The ambulance drove off silently with Chuck in the back. I've got to hurry home to tell Mom and Dad, Deena told herself.

"Thanks for not telling them about the fight," Teddy said to Jade.

"I didn't do it for you," Jade replied wearily.

"Hey, I'm sorry, Jade," Teddy said, shaking his head. "I mean, I thought he had taken something of yours or something. The way you were screaming and chasing after him."

"What were you doing over here in the first place?" Jade demanded.

"I just came over to talk to you," Teddy said, lowering his eyes. "It seems like every time I call you lately, you're too busy to see me."

Jade let out a long sigh. "I'm sorry, Teddy," she said. To Deena's surprise, her friend really did look sorry. "I think you're a terrific guy. But I used to go with Chuck, and now that he's back in town, he's the guy I'm seeing."

"Hey, no problem," Teddy murmured. Even in the darkness Deena could see the disappointment on Teddy's face. He turned quickly and slumped away.

Deena dreaded telling her parents what had happened. But she had no choice.

"Two days he's back, and he's already in trouble!" her father ranted as they drove to Shadyside General.

"Aren't you even worried about him?" Deena cried. "I mean, he's lying in the hospital!"

"Of course I'm worried about him. But what does he expect? Getting into fights all the time!" Mr. Martinson grumbled. "At least he can't get into trouble in the hospital."

"What a *horrible* thing to say!" Deena cried from the backseat.

Mrs. Martinson sighed. "Why can't Chuck just obey the rules like everyone else?"

Deena didn't have an answer. All she knew was that Chuck was Chuck—and he never wanted to be like other people or do the things other people did.

Deena knew that her parents weren't angry with her, but she couldn't help feeling a little guilty. It was almost as though they expected her to keep Chuck out of trouble.

It was a relief when she found Jade waiting for them in the hospital lobby. Deena's parents stopped at the front desk to fill out the insurance forms. Deena and Jade headed straight for Chuck's private room.

They crept into the room. Chuck lay back on his pillows, his face nearly as white as the sheets. Deena had already heard the doctor's report. She knew that Chuck's injuries weren't serious.

But he looked gross. His head was wrapped in a bulky bandage, and his left eye bulged, swollen and bruised.

"Wow! Happy Halloween!" Jade joked.

"Don't make me laugh! I have chapped lips!" Chuck shot back. He groaned. "Did you get the license plate of the truck that hit me?"

Deena and Jade laughed. Forced laughter. Hospital laughter. Sort of hollow and too loud.

"You look great," Chuck told Jade, checking her out with his one good eye.

It was true, Deena realized. Jade *did* look great. She wore a dark green sweater and black jeans. Her hair was pinned up on top of her head, with strands and tendrils hanging below her ears. The male interns and patients had all turned and stared at Jade as she and Deena had walked through the hospital.

"How's your head?" Deena asked.

"Do I still have a head?" Chuck groaned.

"I'm really sorry about what happened," Jade told him, squeezing his hand. "I had no idea Teddy would come over. And I certainly didn't think he'd start a fight."

"He was the guy you were making out with Friday night, right?" Chuck said, not letting her hand go.

"Well, yes," Jade replied reluctantly. "But I told you there's nothing between—"

"I know," Chuck interrupted. "I believe you—now. I guess I didn't before."

"What do you mean?" Jade asked.

For a moment Chuck didn't answer. Then he sighed. "I have something to tell you," he said. His voice came out so weak, Deena had to move up to the bed to hear him. "Something to tell you and Deena."

"What are you talking about?" Deena asked.

"You know those scary phone calls you both got?" Chuck asked. "Well—I know who made them."

"Huh?" Both girls cried out in surprise.

"Who was it?" Deena demanded. "Tell us, Chuck. Who was it?"

chapter

15

"Who was it?" Deena repeated. She had a sinking feeling in her stomach. She knew what Chuck was about to say.

"It was me," Chuck murmured. "I made the calls."

"You creep!" Jade shrieked, pulling her hand from his and backing away from the bed.

"I don't believe it!" Deena uttered. "Why, Chuck? How *could* you?" If he hadn't been lying in a hospital bed, she would have *pounded* him!

"I started making the calls before I came back," Chuck confessed. He stared up at Jade. "A friend of mine from Shadyside told me you were seeing someone else. When I heard that, I went ballistic. I mean, I just stopped thinking straight. All I could think of was how I wanted you to come to L.A. with me. So I decided to scare you."

"Oh, that makes a *lot* of sense!" Jade declared, rolling her eyes.

"But why did you call *me?*" Deena demanded. "I didn't have anything to do with Jade and Teddy."

"I know, Deena, and I'm sorry," Chuck said softly. "The thing is, I thought it would be too obvious if I threatened just Jade. I thought if I called both of you, it would make you think that Farberson was doing it."

"You—you wanted to *terrify* us!" Jade stammered, crossing her arms over her chest.

"That was the idea," Chuck admitted. "I was a jerk, I know." His voice cracked. Deena knew it was never easy for Chuck to apologize.

Jade's eyes narrowed. "Was it also you who sent me that awful note? The one with the bleeding chain saw?"

"Yeah. I sent it," Chuck replied, sighing.

"I don't believe it! I really don't! Are you totally messed up?" Jade fumed. "Why did you think that would make me want to go to California with you?"

"I figured if you thought Farberson was coming after you, you'd want to get as far away from Shadyside as possible." Chuck told her. "I thought you'd *jump* at the opportunity to go to L.A. with me."

"Dumb," Jade snapped, frowning. "Really dumb. The way I feel right now, I wouldn't go across the street with you!"

"I know. I said I'm sorry," Chuck repeated. "I don't know what else to say."

"Well, *thank goodness* Farberson isn't out," Jade declared. "That's the only bit of good news we've had today."

"Whoa. Wait a minute," Deena broke in. "What about that green car? A green car followed us home from school a few days ago. We had to run into an alley to escape it."

"That was me too," Chuck said, groaning. "A friend from the city gave me a ride from the airport. I just wanted to see you, to tell you that I was back. But you ran off before I had the chance."

He reached out to Jade. "Please don't be angry," he begged. "Please accept my apology."

"I'll think about it," Jade replied coldly. Her eyes lit up. "And I'm also going to think of a way to pay you back!"

The next day Deena sat in study hall, staring down at her history notes, trying to force herself to focus. Why am I still so stressed out? she asked herself. Why can't I feel normal and calm again?

She still worried about Chuck. The doctors had kept him in the hospital for observation. They wanted to make sure there was no internal bleeding in his skull.

When she and Jade had left the hospital the night before, Chuck was still talking about his crazy plan to go to Los Angeles. And both Jade and Chuck were still talking excitedly about the money that was supposed to be hidden in Farberson's house.

Why couldn't they forget about it? Deena asked herself. Hadn't they already had enough trouble?

"Deena!" She glanced up, surprised to hear her name, and saw Steve Mason standing beside her. "I've been wanting to talk to you," he whispered.

Deena happily made room for his papers on the table. I've been so wrapped up in Jade and Chuck, I haven't had a moment to think about Steve, Deena thought.

"Is that your research on the Colonial period?" he asked.

Deena nodded. "Yeah. It's for my history term paper."

"Really? I'm working on the same subject in my history class." For the next few moments they whispered about their history papers.

Deena glanced up to see Mr. Raub approaching. "Uh-oh," she said. "Here comes the study-hall cop."

"I've got to get back to my seat anyway," Steve said quickly. "The main reason I wanted to talk to you wasn't the paper. My cousin is giving a party on Friday, and I wondered if you'd like to go with me."

"Sure!" Deena replied, smiling.

"I'll call you tonight," Steve promised. He picked up his papers and hurried back to the other side of the study hall.

* * *

"Good bye, Steve. See you in school tomorrow."

Deena hung up the phone. She couldn't believe it. For the last hour she and Steve had been talking about everything. Australian music, American music, Shadyside, and Sydney, Australia, his hometown. She couldn't remember ever feeling so comfortable with a boy.

Steve and I are going out. At last I have something to look forward to! Deena thought happily. She jumped up from the bed and did a silent dance around her room.

Let Jade and Chuck search for the money in that creepy old house if they want to. As for me—I'm through with the money, through with crazy Chuck and his bad-news plans, through with Farberson, and through with being afraid.

She wandered downstairs to the kitchen, poured herself a glass of orange juice and fixed a plate of crackers and cheese, then took her history book into the TV room. It was her mom's night to work late, and her father was at a meeting. So Deena had the house to herself.

Outside, a freezing mixture of sleet and ice had started to fall, making it feel even cozier inside. She phoned Jade to tell her about Steve, but there was no answer. When Jade's answering machine came on, Deena hung up.

For a few minutes Deena stared at her history notes. Then she switched on the TV. "Might as well have some company," she said aloud.

Bouncy music blared from the TV as a game show ended. Then Deena heard the perky voice of Katy Calloway, a Shadyside news anchor. "A major storm moves into Shadyside. A visitor to town gets a special boost. And a notorious criminal is set free—all on *Channel Five News,* coming up next."

Deena only half listened as several commercials came on. Then she heard the familiar musical theme of the evening news. "Good evening," began the petite woman anchor. "Our top story tonight concerns the release of a notorious Shadyside murderer. For details, let's go to Ralph Browning."

"Thank you, Katy," said Ralph. Deena glanced up to see a handsome blond man standing in front of a prison. Deena lowered her eyes to her homework again.

"I'm at the state prison near Adam Falls," the reporter said. "Earlier today the justices of the State Supreme Court reversed the conviction of a man jailed here last year for the murder of his wife. Because crucial evidence was found to be inadmissible, Stanley Farberson was set free earlier this evening."

"Oh." A frightened moan escaped Deena's throat. She stared into the glare of the TV screen—but couldn't hear another word the reporter said.

Farberson is out! Deena realized. The words repeated in her mind until they became an ugly, frightening chant. *Farberson is out! Out! Out!*

Now what? she asked herself, feeling her entire body shudder.

Will he come after us? Will he come for Jade and me?

Before she had time to think about those questions, the phone rang.

chapter
16

"*H*ello?" Deena answered in a trembling voice.

"Hi, babe."

Deena swallowed hard. "Wh-who is this?" She tried to keep her voice steady. But she stammered out the question shrilly.

"Is Maria there?"

"Huh?" Deena cried. "Who do you want?"

"Oh. Sorry. Wrong number."

Deena heard a click. The dial tone returned.

She replaced the receiver, still feeling shaky. Am I going to be terrified every time the phone rings? she asked herself.

A sudden noise from the kitchen made Deena

jump. Then she realized it was only the refrigerator rumbling on.

Come home, Mom and Dad, she pleaded silently. Please—come home.

Outside, the sleet drummed against the windows with increasing force. The sound made her feel vulnerable. If someone did try to break in, I wouldn't hear them, she realized.

The phone rang again.

"Nooo!" Deena stared at the jangling instrument, terrified. "No. Please." She raised the receiver slowly to her ear. "Hello?"

"Deena!" Jade cried breathlessly at the other end.

Deena let out a sigh of relief. She took a deep breath to force her heart to stop thudding so hard.

"Deena, you'll never guess what happened."

"I saw it!" Deena interrupted. "I saw it on the news."

"Huh? It was on the *news?*" Jade sounded confused. "How would they know about Chuck?"

"Chuck? What's happened with Chuck?" Deena demanded.

"That's what I'm trying to tell you," Jade said impatiently. "After school I went to the hospital. Chuck wasn't in his room, so I sat down to wait. Well, I waited and waited, and finally the nurse came in. She told me he'd checked out!"

"He *what?*" Deena cried in shock. "Chuck *couldn't*

check out, Jade. The doctors told him he'd have to stay in till Tuesday."

"I know," agreed Jade. "The nurse said he left AMA. That means against medical advice."

"My parents are going to *love* this!" Deena muttered glumly.

"He isn't there, is he?" Jade asked.

"Of course not," Deena replied. "But where could he be?"

"He left a message on my answering machine," Jade told her. "Listen to it yourself."

Deena heard a couple of clicks on the other end, and then Chuck's voice, sounding tinny and recorded, came on: "Hey, Jade, it's me. I'm out of the hospital now. If you want to meet me, I'm going over to you-know-where to look for you-know-what. See you later."

"Oh, no!" Deena groaned.

"Oh, *yes!*" Jade replied. "He went to Farberson's house to find the money. Do you believe he'd go over there when he's still injured? Not to mention the major storm we're having."

"We've got bigger worries than the weather!" Deena moaned.

"What do you mean?"

Quickly Deena told Jade what she'd heard on the evening news.

"Huh? They let Farberson out? You can't be serious!" Jade shrieked. "But that's *horrible!*"

"Farberson is probably on his way to his house right now," Deena said, a chill plunging down her back.

Jade fell silent a moment. Deena could almost hear her brain whirring through the line.

"The state prison is near Adam Falls," Jade said finally. "It won't take Farberson more than a couple of hours to get to Shadyside."

"I know, and Chuck is digging around in Farberson's house right now."

"Oh, wow!" Jade said, and became silent all at once. "Chuck. Crazy Chuck," she murmured finally.

"Of course the storm might slow Farberson down," Deena said.

"It doesn't matter," Jade replied. "No matter when he gets home, if he finds Chuck in his house . . ." She didn't finish the sentence.

She didn't have to.

Farberson was a murderer. He had killed once— and gotten away with it.

What would stop him from killing an intruder in his house?

The wind whipped the trees low on the side of the Martinson house. Deena imagined she heard someone at the window.

"Deena—are you there?" Jade asked.

Deena struggled to remain calm. "Of course I'm here."

"Deena, you *know* what we have to do," Jade said softly.

"Yeah. I know," Deena replied in a small voice. "We have to go to Farberson's, don't we? We have to get Chuck out of there before Farberson gets home."

"We don't have a choice," Jade murmured. "We have to save Chuck."

"What if Farberson is already there?" Deena asked.

chapter
____
17

Deena ducked her head against the wind as she headed down her driveway toward the street. She was bundled up in a ski jacket, wool ski hat, and heavy scarf. But the icy wind still stung her face.

Neither she nor Jade could get a car. So they had agreed to meet on the South Shadyside bus.

Deena waited, huddled under the bus shelter, as freezing rain and sleet fell around her. Her teeth chattered while the wind howled and swirled.

She tried to remain calm, but her mind was a confusing jumble of thoughts and fears. How could Chuck do such a foolish thing? she asked herself again and again.

She kept thinking of Farberson, on his way to Fear Street from prison. She could see him again as he had been the year before, fury and madness on his face as he lurched toward Jade and her with his grinding, roaring chain saw.

It'll be okay, Deena, she told herself. You're not going to see Farberson. You're going to find Chuck, get him out of that horrible house. Then the three of you will go back home.

Yes, she assured herself. In another hour we'll all be warm and cozy at home.

At last she saw the bus coming up the hill, its headlights dimmed in the falling sleet.

There were only a few other passengers. Deena took a seat in the back, near the heat. Three stops later Jade climbed on. She was wearing a shiny green parka and matching scarf, with high black boots over her jeans.

As she dropped down beside her friend, Jade unwound the scarf. Deena could see that she had put on makeup, as if she were going on a date!

"I don't believe we're doing this again," Deena said, shivering.

"Me neither," Jade agreed.

"I mean, the only difference is—last time it was raining and this time it's sleeting."

Jade looked around the nearly empty bus. "By the way," she said, "I called Linda Morrison just before I left the house, to make sure she'd heard the news. About Farberson."

"Had she?"

"Her number was disconnected." Jade shrugged. "So I guess she already left town."

"I wish *I* could leave town," Deena muttered.

"Don't worry, Deena," Jade replied softly. "We'll be okay. There hasn't been time for Farberson to get back to Shadyside."

"You hope." Deena sighed. "Why did Chuck have to pick tonight to break out of the hospital and go search for the money?"

Jade didn't reply.

"Maybe Farberson won't go to his house," Deena continued, thinking out loud. "Maybe he'll go to Linda Morrison's instead. Why would he want to go to a cold, deserted house?"

"That makes sense," Jade agreed.

"Sure it does," Deena said, talking herself into it. "And he'll get a big surprise when he finds out she's gone."

"He'll get an even bigger surprise if he goes to his own house and finds Chuck," Jade murmured grimly.

Deena peered out the rain-smeared window into the heavy blackness. "We just passed Canyon Drive. Fear Street is the next stop."

The bus picked up speed on Old Mill Road, swaying with the curves. Neither girl spoke again until it began to slow.

"Here goes," Deena said, sighing. She pressed the bell.

Jade rewound the green scarf around her neck and face, then stood up. "Here goes," she repeated softly.

Nothing to be afraid of, Deena assured herself, stepping off the bus. We have a big head start on

Farberson. We'll be out of here long before he gets to Shadyside. Piece of cake. A piece of cake.

So why did the wind seem so much colder, the sky so much darker on Fear Street? And why did she feel that she was walking to her doom?

"Wait a minute," Jade said. "My scarf is slipping." The girls stepped into a bus shelter while Jade fixed the scarf. "Ready?" she asked when she was once again bundled up.

"Ready as I'll ever be," Deena muttered.

They stepped back out into the driving sleet.

The streetlights cast a dim glow on the cracked sidewalk. The houses on either side of Fear Street were large but run-down. Most of them dark. The bare trees shivered and shook in the swirling wind.

"I'm sure glad I don't live on Fear Street," Jade said in a hushed voice, echoing Deena's thoughts.

The Farberson house loomed ahead in the sleet. To Deena it looked more than ever like a haunted house, with its broken windowpanes, boarded-up windows, and loose shingles.

"I don't see a light," she whispered as they got closer.

"Maybe Chuck is in one of the boarded-up rooms," Jade suggested.

"Or maybe he never went here at all," Deena said. "Maybe—"

"Stop it!" Jade snapped. "Don't start with your *maybes*. Let's just go in and find him—okay?"

The sleet had turned the snow on the lawn into a

sheet of ice. Deena and Jade held on to each other as they crossed the slippery surface.

Both girls were silent climbing the broken steps to the front porch. Jade stepped up to the front door and tried the knob. "Locked," she reported.

"Maybe he's not here," Deena repeated hopefully.

"No *maybes,*" Jade reminded her. "You know Chuck. If he made up his mind to come here to find that money, he's here. The only question is how he got in."

"Maybe he went in through the back door," Deena suggested. Pulling a flashlight from her coat pocket, she aimed the light just ahead of her feet, and led Jade around the back of the house.

"Look!" whispered Jade.

Deena followed her friend's gaze. The back door hung open.

They made their way up to it. Beyond the open door was the kitchen and other rooms, all dark as the inside of a tomb.

"How do you suppose Chuck got it open?" Deena whispered.

"Maybe he found it that way," Jade replied. "Come on."

"What if it wasn't Chuck who opened it?" Deena demanded, holding back. "What if it was Farberson?"

"Farberson couldn't have gotten here so fast, not in this storm," Jade insisted. "Now, come on, let's go in before we freeze to death."

Holding her breath, Deena followed Jade into the

kitchen. Her flashlight highlighting the linoleum smeared with dirt. "Jade—" Deena started.

"Shhh!" Jade instructed. "Be quiet. Let's see if we can hear anything."

Both girls stood frozen by the doorway, listening. But there was no sound, except for the rush of the wind and the pounding of the sleet against the walls and windows.

"I don't hear a thing," Deena whispered. "I think the house is empty."

"Let's look around," Jade suggested.

Gingerly, Deena stepped farther into the kitchen. She aimed her light around the small room. "Wow," she murmured. "This place is a wreck."

A year ago the house had been messy. But now it was a disaster area. Cans, bottles, dishes, pots, and pans were strewn everywhere, along with empty, crushed boxes of cereal, flour, and rice. Deena shuddered as her light swept over small animal footprints on the floor.

"I don't think the Farbersons were such good housekeepers," Jade joked.

"I bet Linda did all this," Deena replied. "When she was searching for the money."

"She was thorough," Jade said. "She searched everything."

Deena kept the flashlight beam aimed ahead of her as they moved into the living room. This room was even more torn apart than the kitchen.

Furniture had been overturned. Books and pillows

littered the floor. The sofa had been cut open and its stuffing pulled out and tossed all over.

Deena spotted a faint brown stain on the rug near the hallway. She moved the light away. She remembered it was the place where they had discovered Mrs. Farberson's stabbed body.

"There are more rooms downstairs, aren't there?" Jade asked.

Deena tried to remember the house. "There's a dining room and I think there's a closet over next to the stairs," she replied.

She cautiously opened the dark wood door next to the stairs, to reveal a hot-water heater and several pieces of luggage, all ripped open.

"I wonder if she tore everything apart upstairs," Jade said after they searched the dining room.

"Probably," Deena replied. "She told us she'd been all through the house."

Deena had breathed a little easier as they finished wandering through the downstairs rooms. But now, as they started up the creaky wooden stairs, she felt panic rising again. Each time she placed her foot on a creaking step, she remembered the sound of Farberson climbing the stairs to get them last year.

They stopped halfway up the stairs. "Why don't we hear Chuck moving around?" Jade wondered out loud.

"Maybe he's deliberately keeping silent. Maybe he hears *us* and thinks we're here to stop him," Deena suggested.

"Maybe," Jade agreed. "Chuck!" she suddenly called. "Chuck, it's us! Jade and Deena!"

No answer.

They made their way up to the landing. Deena couldn't see light from any of the upstairs rooms. The air felt even colder on the second floor. "I don't think I've ever been so cold in my life!" she complained, shivering.

"Just keep moving," Jade instructed. "Chuck!" she called again. "Chuck, are you up here?"

Silence.

"No one here," Deena murmured. "Maybe he already found the money and left."

"Maybe," Jade said. "Come on, let's check out the bedrooms."

The first bedroom had been Stanley Farberson's office. Deena felt her stomach turn over as she recognized the beat-up desk, the overturned file cabinets, and the closet where she and Jade had hidden.

"Yuck. This brings back bad memories," Jade whispered.

"It looks like someone has gone through all this stuff," Deena replied, sweeping her light over the room. "There's no way to tell if it was Linda Morrison or Chuck."

"It might have been both of them," said Jade. "But no one's here now—at least not in this room."

The next room had a broken card table leaning against one wall. No other furniture. The closet was dark and empty. Someone had cut through the wallpaper with something sharp.

They stepped into a tiny bedroom. It looked as if it might have been a guest room, with a single bed and a low, two-drawer dresser.

Jade kneeled down and searched under the bed. Nothing there.

"We're running out of rooms," Deena whispered.

"One more," Jade replied grimly. "I'm sure you remember it."

Deena nodded. She could never forget the fourth bedroom. Farberson had trapped them in that room when he'd discovered them hiding in the house.

The room was a complete wreck. The contents of the dressers had been emptied onto the floor, and the mattress had been slashed open.

A tall pile of trash had been shoved against the closet door. Deena kicked it aside. She swept her light into the closet.

Empty. Except for a heap of women's clothes on the floor.

"Chuck's not here," she told Jade. "In fact, I don't think he ever came."

Jade sighed. "When he left the hospital, he must have decided the weather was too awful to travel here."

Deena uttered an angry growl. "He's probably home safe and warm—while we're here freezing to death. I'll *kill* Chuck when I see him."

Jade giggled. "Not if I get my hands on him first!"

Deena felt as if a weight had been lifted from her shoulders.

"I can't wait to get home," Jade said. "I'm going to take the hottest bath I can, and drink about a gallon of cocoa."

"Great idea," Deena said. "So what are we waiting for?"

She was already halfway down the hall, making her way quickly toward the stairs, when Jade's voice stopped her. "Deena—come back. Check this out!"

"Huh?" Deena turned around, the light bobbing in front of her.

"I just found this on the floor," Jade said. "It looks like—oh, no!"

Deena lowered the light to Jade's hand. She was holding a clear, flat plastic ring.

It took Deena a few seconds to recognize it.

She gasped when she finally realized it was an ID bracelet, the kind hospitals give to patients.

Trembling, Deena took the bracelet and examined it. A wave of fear swept over her. She already knew what the bracelet would say. But a hard shudder shook her body as she read: "Charles B. Martinson."

"He's here!" Jade breathed. "Or at least he *was* here."

"But where?" Deena cried, uselessly searching the room.

No sign Chuck had been here. No sign anyone had been here, except for . . .

Deena's flashlight stopped on the bare floor in front

of the closet. In the quivering circle of light she saw several dark stains.

Deena hesitated. But Jade hurried to the closet and knelt down. She stuck out a finger, rubbed it on the floor.

In the white light from the flashlight, the tip of Jade's finger came up red.

She gazed up at Deena, her face twisted in horror. "It's blood," Jade whispered.

chapter

18

A strong wind rattled the windowpanes. Then Deena heard another sound.

A soft rustling.

"Did you hear that?" she asked Jade in a whisper.

Jade listened hard. "Hear what?"

"There it is again," Deena insisted. "I think it's coming from inside the closet."

"Huh? We searched the closet," Jade replied.

Taking a deep breath, Deena stepped around Jade and pulled the closet door all the way open.

Nothing in there.

Just the pile of women's clothing. Sweaters and skirts.

"Ohhhh." Deena let out a moan as the clothing started to move.

"Deena—what is it?" Jade moved up behind her.

They both stared in shock as the skirts and sweaters began to rise.

Two arms shot out from under the clothes. Someone groaned. "Deena. Jade. Is that you?"

The clothing fell away. Chuck raised himself to a sitting position on the closet floor. He stared up, squinting against the beam of light. His forehead was bruised, and a wide smear of blood covered the right side of his head.

"Chuck!" Deena managed to choke out.

"What are you *doing* in there?" Jade demanded. "What happened?"

"Where is it?" he groaned, rubbing the wound on the side of his head.

"Where is *what?*" Jade demanded.

"The money! Someone took the money!" He pushed himself to his knees and started to stand up. But he instantly sat down again, holding his head.

"There's no money here," Deena insisted. "What are you talking about?"

"I found it," Chuck mumbled groggily.

"You found what?" Jade cried. "You found the money?"

He nodded, still squinting, still rubbing his head. "It was in a metal box under the floorboards. I pulled it out. But then I heard a noise."

"What happened?" Jade asked.

"That's the last thing I remember," Chuck groaned.

He leaned back against the wall of the closet. "Some-one must have hit me and taken it."

"Let's talk about it later," Deena urged. "We've got to get out of here."

Both girls knelt beside Chuck. The hospital bandage around his head had come half unwrapped. Beneath it, Deena could see the stitches from the wound he had received in the fight with Teddy. Next to the stitches she saw a new cut oozing blood into his hair.

"You're still bleeding," Jade told him softly. She took an edge of her scarf and tenderly dabbed at the blood.

"Come on, Chuck," Deena urged. "Get up. We'll help you."

Leaning heavily on both girls, he managed to stand up. He took a deep breath. "Wow! What a headache!" he cried.

"No wonder," Deena told him. "You have another big cut on your head."

"So what happened?" Jade asked as they awkwardly made their way into the hallway.

"I hitched a ride from the hospital," Chuck reported. "When I got here, it was still light out. The kitchen door was unlocked, so I came in. Then I started searching for the money, but everything was trashed and ripped apart."

"Tell me about it," Jade murmured.

"Anyway," Chuck continued as they helped him down the hall, "I tried to think of a weird place

Farberson might have hidden the money. Someplace his girlfriend hadn't thought of."

"Where would that be?" Deena exclaimed. "She even ripped off the wallpaper in some of the rooms."

Halfway down the hall, Deena stopped.

What was that sound? Footsteps downstairs?

No. Just the old house creaking in the strong wind.

"So where did you look?" Jade asked.

"I realized that Morrison had searched everywhere but the floor," Chuck replied, sounding stronger. "So I started going through the house room by room, searching for any floorboards that seemed loose, or didn't seem to match the others."

"And?" Deena asked eagerly.

"It took me a really long time," Chuck continued. "Finally, in the closet of the last bedroom, I found two floorboards that didn't quite match. The wood seemed to be newer.

"I found a letter opener in the desk in the other room. I used it to pry the boards up. And there it was." He stopped for a moment and leaned against the wall. "All hundred- and five-hundred-dollar bills. I never saw so much money in my life! It was awesome!"

"And someone hit you and took it!" Jade exclaimed.

Chuck nodded. "I guess."

"Farberson," Deena said firmly. "Farberson was here already."

"Huh? What are you talking about?" Chuck demanded, squinting hard at her.

They told Chuck about Farberson's release from prison. "That's why we're here," Deena finished. "We came to warn you."

"How long ago did he get out?" Chuck demanded.

"We're not positive," Deena replied. "Come on. We've got to hurry."

But Jade held back, her features tight. "He could still be here," she murmured. "Farberson could still be in this house."

"Cool!" Chuck cried. "Then I could punch out his lights and take the money back from him!"

"Are you crazy?" Deena wailed. "Chuck, you can hardly walk. Farberson probably has a gun. He nearly killed us once. Let's just get out of this house and go home!"

"Let's get out before he has a chance to come back," Jade urged.

"All right. All right," Chuck said grudgingly. "I'm still a little dizzy. Let's go."

"Lean on me," Jade instructed. She put one arm around Chuck's waist and began to help him down the stairs.

Deena made her way quickly to the living room. As she looked back to Chuck and Jade, it seemed as if they were moving in slow motion.

What if Farberson *was* still in the house?

"Come on, guys—hurry!" she pleaded.

"We're going as fast as we can," Jade called down. "We don't want Chuck to suddenly faint or something."

"I'm feeling steadier," Chuck said. They reached the bottom of the stairs. Deena saw him pull away from Jade. "I can walk on my own now," he reported.

They made their way through the darkness to the kitchen. Stepping over the trash on the floor, Deena thought, I hope I never, never, never see this horrible house again!

And then a light flared. Yellow light. Outside the kitchen door. Flickering in through the filthy window.

"Someone's out there!" Chuck exclaimed.

They ducked behind the kitchen counter as the door opened.

Wind howled into the room.

The light revealed the silhouette of a tall, heavy man.

The silhouette of Stanley Farberson.

chapter
19

Deena's legs turned to rubber. Her entire body shuddered.

Farberson stood in the doorway, his stern features reflected in the glow of a big camp lantern.

"Quick!" Chuck whispered, and shoved them through a door right behind them.

"Careful!" he cautioned after he silently pulled the door shut. "It's a stairway to the basement."

Huddling on the landing, Deena heard Farberson lumber into the house. She stood squeezed between her brother and the wall, terrified, almost afraid to breathe. Behind her she could feel the damp chill of the basement.

She glanced at Jade on the other side of Chuck. Jade stared straight ahead at the door, stiff as a mannequin.

Farberson's heavy footsteps came nearer.

Was he going to pull open the basement door and find them standing there?

No. The footsteps faded. Into another room.

Why did he come back? Deena wondered. He already has the money. What made him come back to this dump?

"Let's go downstairs," Chuck whispered. "There's got to be a way out from there."

He took the flashlight from Deena and aimed it on the stairs. They were old and splintered. Several steps were missing.

They made their way down slowly. Deena ignored the scuttling sounds, the pittering of tiny feet.

The rats can run around all they want, she thought, shivering. I'm going to be out of here in seconds.

The basement came dimly into view as Chuck swept the beam of light along the walls and floor. Trash cluttered every inch—rags, papers, machinery parts, a shovel without a handle. Along the walls, battered cardboard cartons reached to the ceiling.

"I don't see a window," Jade cried, her voice shaking.

"There's got to be one!" Chuck declared. "Follow me."

A loud noise behind them made them freeze.

It's him! Deena realized.

The sound repeated. She raised her eyes to the basement ceiling. Farberson was walking above them.

He'll leave soon, she told herself. He'll find what he

came for—and he'll leave. And then the three of us can leave too.

"Come on," Chuck urged. "Where's a window?"

The clomping footsteps stopped.

"I think he's gone," Jade whispered, eyes raised to the low ceiling.

"Probably went upstairs," Chuck replied, listening hard. "Don't think about him. Let's find a way out of here." Once again he swept the flashlight around the dark, cluttered basement.

"Isn't that a window back there?" Jade asked. She pointed to the back wall, where the old cartons were piled the highest.

Deena squinted and could see it too—a dark rectangle peeking out from behind a stack of cartons.

They hurried to the back wall. "Come on," Chuck urged. "Let's move the boxes."

The top box was too high to pull down. Chuck piled two cartons beside the tall stack. Then he climbed up on them.

As Deena and Jade held his legs steady, he reached up—reached—reached—

"Look out!" he cried.

Deena and Jade stumbled back as the carton toppled to the basement floor.

"You okay?" Chuck called, jumping down. "It was so heavy. It slipped out of my hands."

"What if Farberson heard that?" Deena wondered out loud.

They listened.

Silence. Except for the wind battering the house.

"With the carton out of the way, can we get to the window?" Deena asked.

"Let's see." Chuck boosted himself over the pile of boxes and climbed up to the window. A moment later he dropped back down to the floor. "No way," he said glumly. "It's painted shut. And it's too small to climb through anyway."

"But it's the only window!" Jade cried, her face pale in the flashlight's glow.

"That means we're trapped here," Deena said. All at once she felt hopeless. Last year was repeating itself. They were trapped here, here in this frightening house, trapped with a killer.

"Take it easy, Deena," Chuck told her. "The basement's a dead end. So we'll just go back up through the house."

"Are you crazy?" cried Deena. "He's up there."

"It's a big house," Chuck replied. "Farberson is probably upstairs. It's only a few feet to the kitchen door. All we have to do is make sure the coast is clear, and make a run for it."

"I—I guess," Deena stammered.

"Hurry," Chuck urged. "Let's go back up."

"Chuck," Jade whispered, grabbing his arm. "Better turn off the flashlight. He might see it shining under the door."

"Good thinking," Chuck agreed. He clicked off the light.

Deena shuddered at the thought of climbing the rotted stairs in the dark. But she knew Jade was right.

They slowly pulled themselves up, leaning on the narrow banister.

They were nearly to the top when the door swung open and a bright light washed over them.

"Who's there?" Farberson bellowed.

His eyes narrowed as he studied them. And then an unpleasant smile spread over his round face.

"A welcoming party!" he croaked, laughing. "You shouldn't have. Really. You *shouldn't* have."

chapter
20

Deena couldn't take her eyes off Farberson. He had changed a lot in the past year.

He was dressed in a faded blue shirt and baggy gray trousers. His face, covered in a growth of whiskers, was leaner. Dark circles ringed his eyes.

"Get out of our way!" Chuck demanded, stepping in front of Jade and Deena. "Let us out of here."

Farberson didn't budge. He shook his head, his smile fading slowly. "Are you for real, kid?"

"I mean it!" Chuck insisted. He took another step up the stairs.

"Not one more step," Farberson said softly. Deena saw something gleam in the man's hand. A small automatic pistol.

He raised it slowly and gestured with it. "Downstairs, everyone," he instructed. "Quickly."

"Wh-what are you going to do?" Deena choked out.

Was he going to shoot all three of them and leave them in the basement? Had he been thinking about them all the time he was in prison, planning to take his revenge?

He didn't answer Deena. "Hurry, everyone. Watch your step," he called almost cheerfully.

Chuck scowled and started to resist. Then Deena saw his expression change. He sighed and led the way back down to the dark, cluttered basement.

"Good," Farberson said when they had reached the bottom of the steps. He stood a few steps above them, holding the gun steady in his hand.

"All right," he said. "This won't take long."

He raised the pistol and aimed it at Deena.

chapter

21

The gun gleamed in the lantern light. Farberson held it steady in his right hand, pointed at Deena's chest. His eyes moved from Deena to Jade to Chuck.

"I think I've got your attention," he said, snickering. "Let's make this short and sweet, okay?" He cleared his throat. "Just tell me where it is."

"Tell you where *what* is?" Jade demanded in a quivering voice.

"Don't play games," Farberson replied without any emotion. "The money. Just tell me where the money is, and I'll let you go."

"Huh? The money? But we don't know where it is!" Jade insisted.

"Why are you asking us?" Chuck broke in. "You took it!"

Farberson stared at Chuck thoughtfully. He moved the pistol so that it was aiming at Chuck's chest. "I'm very disappointed," he murmured. "I don't like games. I really don't. It's been a long night, and I'm sure you'd like to go home, right? So tell me where the money is."

"We don't have it!" Deena cried. "That's the truth!"

"Then why are you here?" Farberson demanded. "What are you doing in my house?"

No one spoke.

Deena glanced at Chuck and Jade. They looked as frightened as she felt.

Finally Chuck broke the silence with a long sigh. "Okay, okay," he told Farberson. "We came here to look for the money. At least, I did. But I don't have it. That's the truth. I swear." He raised his right hand as if taking an oath.

"You're a bad liar, son," Farberson replied.

"I'm not lying!" Chuck protested.

"If you didn't take the money, then where is it?" Farberson demanded. "It's not where I hid it."

"Maybe—maybe someone else took it," Deena suggested in a choked, frightened voice.

"Like who?" Farberson shot back. "The tooth fairy?"

"We don't have it!" Chuck cried. "We—"

"I told you I don't like games," Farberson said,

stepping into the basement. "I told you I'd let you leave as soon as you told me the truth."

"But—but we are!" Deena sputtered.

"I bet I can make you tell me the truth," Farberson said grimly. He pointed the gun at Deena. "You!" he barked, startling her by raising his voice for the first time.

"I—I don't know anything!" Deena stammered.

"Go over to that workbench," he ordered, gesturing to a litter-covered table against one wall. "You'll find rope there. Bring it over here."

Deena continued to stare at him.

"Now!" he snapped, raising the gun as if to hit her.

Deena turned and stumbled in the darkness over to the far wall. The bench was covered with rusted tools, stacks of papers, and stained rags. At one end of the table she found some short coils of rope.

"Here," she said, handing the rope to Farberson.

"Good," he snapped. He took one of the lengths and tossed it back to Deena. "Take the rope and tie up buddy-boy here." He squinted at Chuck. "What happened to your head, kid? A truck run over it?"

"I got in a fight," Chuck muttered, feeling his wound. *"And* someone just knocked me out."

"Guess I'm not the only one who doesn't like you," Farberson growled. "Aren't you hurting enough? Don't you want to tell me the truth about my money so I don't have to mess you up more?"

"I *told* you—" Chuck started to say.

"Tie up his hands and feet," Farberson ordered Deena.

"No—please!" Deena begged.

Farberson waved the pistol. "It's got real bullets in it," he said dryly. "I know you kids think this is some kind of Nancy Drew adventure story, but it's not. It's all real. And if I don't get my money, I'm really going to hurt you."

Deena swallowed hard. She realized that she had no choice.

Chuck turned around and clasped his hands behind his back. Deena began winding the rope around them. She made the knots as loose as possible while pretending to pull them tight.

When she'd finished binding Chuck's hands, she turned to Farberson. "Should I do his feet now?"

"Just a minute," Farberson snarled. He set his lantern on the floor and walked over to Deena and Chuck. He tugged at the rope around Chuck's hands.

"Too loose!" he fumed. "Do you think I'm a moron?" Before Deena could back away, Farberson lashed out and slapped her across the face with the back of his hand. "Now do it right!" he demanded.

Deena staggered back against the wall. Blinking back tears, she tried to ignore the stinging pain and unwound the ropes. With trembling hands she retied them, tighter this time.

It took only a few minutes to bind Chuck and Jade. Now they were seated side by side on the cold floor, their backs against the wall, helpless, unable to move their hands or feet.

"Good job," Farberson said solemnly. "Now you." He slid the gun into his pants pocket and grabbed Deena's hand.

She tried to pull away. But he was much stronger.

He jerked her arm so hard, she felt it was coming out of the socket. "I can make this easier," he threatened. "I can knock you out."

Deena stopped struggling and stood meekly while Farberson tied her hands together. He shoved her down on the floor and tied her feet next. Then he pushed her against the wall beside Jade.

Deena tried to stay in control, to fight the tears that threatened to flow. The ropes bit into her wrists and ankles.

Farberson stared at them grimly. "I really don't have time for this," he muttered. "Does anyone want to save us all a lot of trouble and pain? Anyone want to tell me where my money is?"

"For the last time," Chuck pleaded in a hoarse, frightened voice. "We don't know!"

"We'll see," Farberson replied, frowning. "I guess we'll see in a few minutes what you know and don't know."

Whistling a tuneless melody, he crossed to the other side of the basement, where most of the tools were piled. Through the gloom Deena could see him rummaging around in the piles of junk.

Then he straightened up and came lumbering back to them.

He was carrying something in each hand.

Deena shut her eyes and let out a frightened cry when she saw what he was carrying.

A gallon can of gasoline.

And a chain saw.

chapter

22

When Deena opened her eyes, she saw Jade twisting at her ropes, struggling to burst free. Chuck stared straight ahead. But Deena caught the fear on his face, saw his chin quivering as Farberson bent over the ugly chain saw.

"I wonder if it still cuts," Farberson murmured more to himself than to his prisoners.

Deena shuddered. She could still remember her terror a year earlier, when Farberson had come after her and Jade with the saw. How helpless they had felt, trapped high in a tree. How the tree had begun to shake as the whirring saw cut into it.

"Give us a break!" Chuck exclaimed. "We told you everything we know. I looked for the money. But I didn't find it!"

"We'll see," Farberson replied calmly. "Let me get my lie detector running here."

"Please!" Jade begged. "Please let us go! We won't tell anyone we saw you. We—we'll help you look for the money!" she volunteered.

"Yes!" Deena chimed in. "That's right. We'll help you look for it."

Ignoring them, Farberson opened the can of gasoline. Then he tilted it over the chain saw's tank.

The gasoline made a *glug, glug, glug* sound as it flowed into the saw.

Deena suddenly pictured her room at home. So warm. So comfortable. So—safe.

I wonder if I'll ever see it again, she thought. A loud sob escaped her throat.

Farberson glanced up. "Were you volunteering to go first?" he asked Deena.

"No. I—" Deena started to say. But her voice cracked. She felt hot tears rolling down her cheeks.

"Okay. I think the lie detector is ready," Farberson told her. "You can go first."

He tugged at the rope. The chain saw coughed but didn't start.

Please don't start! Deena begged silently. *Please don't work!*

But with a second tug of the rope, the chain saw roared to life.

At the sound of the grinding whine, Deena felt her stomach lurch. When she and Jade had been imprisoned in the tree, the grinding, ear-jarring roar had been the most terrifying part of their ordeal.

The chain saw's shrill whine echoed through the dark basement. As if hypnotized, Deena stared at it, stared at the whirling chain, the sharp, rotating teeth.

"You've got to believe us!" Deena wailed, tears sliding down her cheeks. But she knew that Farberson couldn't hear her above the roar.

Farberson's face was set in determination, his eyes narrowed. He cut through the air with the saw, swooping it low over Deena's feet.

Deena pressed back against the stone wall. Her entire body rigid as if she had died, as if she were already stiffening up.

Farberson swooped the roaring saw down again. Deena shut her eyes.

Is he really going to cut us?

Why won't he believe us?

Farberson bent low, his face hovering over Deena's, so low she could smell onions on his breath. "Do you want to tell me now?" he shouted. "Where is it? Where is the money?"

"I don't know!" Deena screamed. "I really don't know!"

"Think hard!" he bellowed. "Does this help you think?" He brought the saw high up in the air, then began to lower it.

Deena couldn't move. Couldn't blink. Couldn't take her eyes from the whirring teeth of the blade.

"Tell me!" Farberson demanded furiously. "Someone tell me where the money is! Tell me now, or I'll cut her! I'll cut her bad!"

"Stop it!" Chuck yelled.

Jade let out a horrified shriek. The shrill sound blending with the whine of the chain saw.

Slowly, slowly Farberson lowered the saw toward Deena's shoulder.

chapter
23

*D*eena opened her mouth to scream, but no sound came out.

The saw loomed so near, she could feel the hot air from its whirring chain.

She pressed her back hard into the stone wall, trying to disappear into the wall. The whining roar cut through her mind, sharp as the teeth on the hovering chain saw.

Farberson lowered the saw. Closer. Closer. So close she could see every detail of his hands. She could see the hair on the back of his hand, the dirt under his fingernails, the white marks across his knuckles as he squeezed tight on the handle.

He's going to cut me, Deena knew.

He isn't faking. He's going to cut me now.

She shut her eyes as the grinding roar vibrated her entire body.

"Stop!"

Chuck's desperate cry from beside her.

"Stop!"

Deena opened her eyes.

Farberson raised the saw an inch. Two inches.

"Don't hurt her!" Chuck screamed. "I'll tell you the truth!"

Farberson straightened up. He held the saw over Deena, but he shifted his gaze to Chuck.

"Please stop!" Chuck repeated. "I'll tell you everything I know."

"I'm waiting," shouted Farberson.

"First move away from her!" Chuck demanded.

"You aren't in any position to bargain!" Farberson replied sharply. "Now, tell me where the money is!"

"I don't know where it is," Chuck began, "but—"

"No good!" Farberson shouted. He turned and lowered the chain saw over Deena.

Deena screamed.

"Wait!" Chuck yelled. "Listen to me!"

Farberson's face reflected his disgust. He switched the chain saw off.

The silence seemed as loud as the chain saw's roar.

Deena sucked in a deep breath. Tears rolled down her cheeks. Her chest heaved. Her entire body trembled.

Beside her, she heard Jade sobbing.

"All right," Farberson demanded. "Let's hear it."

141

"You were right," Chuck told him. "I came here to look for the money. And—the truth is that I found it."

"Where?" Farberson demanded. A crafty smile had spread over his face.

"In the last bedroom upstairs," Chuck said. "In the closet, under some loose floorboards."

Farberson shifted slightly. His entire attention was now on Chuck. "So where is it?" he demanded.

"I don't know," Chuck told him.

Farberson made a snarling noise and moved the chain saw in his hands.

Desperately Chuck added, "Someone hit me and took it! When I woke up, I was lying in the closet. And the money was gone!"

For a moment Farberson stared at Chuck. Then he shook his head. "You found the money—and someone else stole it?" he said sarcastically. "This house sure is crowded tonight!"

"That's what's happened!" Chuck insisted shrilly.

Farberson shook his head. "No way I'm going to believe that," he growled.

"It's the truth!" Chuck cried. "I found it. I had it in my hands. But someone took it from me."

"I guess you don't care so much about your friend after all!" Farberson snapped.

"I'm telling you the *truth!*" Chuck insisted, pleading.

"You know what?" said Farberson. "I don't care if

it is. I don't have my money. But I do have you—exactly where I want you."

He shifted the chain saw. "You've been nothing but trouble to me," he growled. "Everything that's happened has been your fault!"

"Wait!" Chuck cried.

But Farberson wasn't listening. His eyes grew wide with excitement. His face tightened. With a hard yank he started up the saw again.

Deena stared up in terror as Farberson hovered over her again. She could see the wild glow in his eyes.

He's gone over the edge! she realized.

He doesn't even care about the money. He doesn't care what he does to us.

He wants revenge.

Farberson inched closer. Closer still.

The shrill whine of the blade cut through Deena's mind.

The whirring teeth lowered toward her throat.

He isn't going to stop this time, Deena knew.

He isn't going to stop.

chapter

24

Deena shut her eyes. Every muscle in her body tightened.

The chain saw roared louder.

Then was turned off.

Huh? What's going on? she wondered.

She opened her eyes to see Farberson staring up at the top of the stairs.

"Hey!" Farberson screamed, startled.

Her entire body trembling, her chest heaving, Deena raised her eyes to the stairs.

At first all she saw was the beam of white from a flashlight.

As her eyes adjusted, a figure came into view. A dark raincoat. A sleeve moved. A gloved hand.

The hand held a silvery pistol.

The pistol was pointed at Farberson.

"Put down the saw, Stanley." Deena recognized the voice. Then she saw Linda Morrison's stern face as the woman made her way down the stairs.

Oh, thank goodness! Deena told herself.

Farberson turned away from Deena to face Linda Morrison. "What are *you* doing here?" he demanded, quickly getting over his surprise.

"Who is that?" Deena heard Chuck whisper to Jade.

"It's Linda," Jade whispered back. "Linda Morrison!"

Linda stepped onto the basement floor. She motioned with the pistol. "Drop the saw," she repeated. "And move away from my friends."

Farberson kept the chain saw waist-high. "Your friends, huh?" he murmured. He lowered his gaze to her pistol. "That little gun doesn't scare me, Linda. I don't think you'd shoot me."

"Try me," she challenged.

Farberson squinted at her, thinking hard.

She moved steadily toward him, kicking empty cartons and garbage out of her path. "You're not going to hurt my friends," she said softly.

Farberson turned uncertainly, then began to back up toward the opposite wall. "Linda—what's your problem?" he demanded. "I thought that you and I—"

She took another step toward him. "Put down the saw, Stanley. I'm not going to warn you again."

Deena swallowed hard as she watched them. It was as if they were involved in some kind of weird dance. With every step she took forward, he took one back. He was still holding the chain saw with both hands. But the anger had faded from his face, replaced now by fear.

Thank goodness she came to save us, Deena thought. If she had come a few seconds later . . .

But Deena realized she and Jade and Chuck weren't safe yet. First Linda Morrison had to do something about Farberson.

"I'm going to count to five," Linda told him sternly. "If you don't drop the chain saw, I'll shoot you, Stanley."

He snickered. "You're kidding, right? This is a joke. You can't be pals with these kids." He took another step back, his eyes locked on the pistol in her hand.

"One," she said.

He backed up another step, bumping a stack of cartons. "Let's get serious, okay, Linda? You and I—"

"Two," she counted.

"Linda, please—" Now Farberson was begging.

"Three," she answered, her voice hard and cold.

Is she really going to shoot him? Deena wondered, watching the tense scene without blinking, without breathing. Morrison had been in love with him. Would she really shoot him now?

"Let me explain—" Farberson pleaded, taking another step back.

"Time's running out, Stanley," she replied calmly. "Four."

"Linda—give me a break," he muttered. "This is stupid. Let's you and I—"

"Five!" she shouted. She raised the gun.

"All right!" Farberson cried. "You win! I'll put it down!"

He swung the chain saw down.

But instead of lowering it to the floor, he gave the rope a hard jerk.

With a deafening roar, the saw whirred to life.

Morrison cried out angrily.

Farberson raised the grinding saw—and dove toward her.

Deena gasped as she saw Farberson stumble.

He fell over a carton.

The saw slipped out of his grasp and clattered onto the concrete floor.

He shot out his hands. His eyes wild.

He grabbed at air.

And fell onto the roaring saw.

The shrill whine of the cutting teeth drowned out Farberson's scream.

The whirring chain cut through his chest. Deena turned away sickened.

Then silence.

A heavy, cold silence.

"He's dead," Linda Morrison murmured, standing over Farberson's body, sprawled facedown over the saw. "Stanley is dead."

The horror is over, Deena thought gratefully. We're okay. We're going to be okay.

"I can't believe he's gone," Morrison said, sighing.

"It—it was an accident," Deena stammered. "We all know you didn't mean it to happen."

Morrison stepped away from the body and turned to Deena. "No," she said softly. "Not an accident."

"Huh?" Deena glanced at Jade, who was still trembling, tears running down her cheeks.

"Not an accident," Morrison repeated. "I planned to kill Stanley. That's why I came back. He just made it easier for me."

She sighed and slapped the barrel of the gun against her gloved hand. Then she raised her eyes to Deena, Jade, and Chuck. "Now I just have to figure out what to do with you," she said.

chapter

25

"I'm afraid you've become a problem," Linda Morrison said, frowning.

"You don't need to worry about us," Chuck spoke up. "We saw what happened. Farberson fell. It was his own fault. A total accident."

"Who's going to believe that?" Morrison snapped. "Besides, if he hadn't killed himself, I would have shot him—and he knew it."

"But I thought you were so afraid of him," Jade cried. "I thought you said he threatened you."

"I was afraid of him," Morrison replied. "I had good reason to be. He knew I wanted the money. And I knew he'd do anything to keep me from getting it."

She began pacing back and forth. Deena stared hard

at her. She was wearing a stylish new raincoat. She had carefully made up her face and had a new hairdo.

"Wow. I get it," Chuck declared. "You were the one who hit me on the head and took the money."

"Congratulations," Morrison replied sarcastically. "What a whiz kid."

"You mean *you* have the money?" Jade asked.

"I have it right here," Morrison said, patting the pocket of her raincoat. "I also have a plane ticket for someplace warm and far, far away."

"But—but how did you know I'd find the money upstairs?" Chuck demanded, sounding very confused. "How did you know I was here?"

"Believe me," Morrison confided, "you were the *last* person I expected to find. For months I searched this dump. But I couldn't find the money. Then I heard this afternoon that Stanley was released from prison. I knew he'd come here like a shot to get his money.

"So I drove here to wait for him," Morrison continued. "My plan was to hide, wait for Stanley to get the money, then take it from him. But I found *you* here instead!" She pointed at Chuck with the pistol. "You already found the money." She chuckled. "My lucky day, I guess."

"You hit Chuck and took the money," Jade said. "So why'd you come back here?"

"To kill Stanley, of course," Morrison replied casually. "I didn't want to spend the rest of my life worrying that he might find me."

"But why?" Deena started.

"Enough talk," Morrison snapped. "I have an unpleasant errand to do now."

She turned, shining her flashlight over the walls and the cluttered floor. "Perfect," she murmured. She crossed to the other side of the basement and began gathering up some of the old rags scattered across the floor.

"What are you doing?" Deena asked, feeling a chill down her back.

"Getting some kindling together," Morrison replied casually. "I want a nice, bright fire. And old rags burn so well."

She placed the rags in a pile on the workbench, then crossed the room for more rags from the trash on the floor.

When she had a tall pile of rags, she picked up Farberson's gasoline can. Then she raised it and began to sprinkle gasoline over the rags.

"No!" Deena shrieked. "Let us go! We won't tell anyone! We won't—"

"You can trust us," Chuck said with conviction. "We have no reason to tell anyone. You don't have to set a fire. By the time someone finds us, you'll be far away."

For a moment Linda seemed to consider Chuck's words. Then she went back to pouring gasoline on the rags. "Sorry," she told them. "I don't feel like taking chances."

Deena leaned toward Jade. "Keep her talking," she whispered. "Maybe we can stall her."

"Did you know about the money all along?" Jade asked. "I mean, last year, before Farberson killed his wife?"

Linda snickered. "Did I know?" she exclaimed. "The whole thing was my idea. Remember, I was the bookkeeper at Stanley's restaurant. I got him to steal money from the restaurant and then I got him to kill his wife." She shook her head. "He was stupid. He did everything I told him."

I don't believe this, Deena thought. Linda Morrison was actually responsible for everything that had happened last year.

"I'm sorry, kids," Morrison said. "But it's show time."

"Wait—please!" Deena begged.

"There won't be much left for the police to find," Morrison said, ignoring Deena's plea. "But there should be enough to make it look as if Stanley tied you up and then had an unfortunate accident with the chain saw."

She reached into her raincoat pocket—and pulled out a lighter.

chapter

26

Deena watched, frozen in horror, as Linda Morrison fumbled around on Farberson's worktable, searching for something.

What is she looking for? Deena wondered, unable to stop her body from trembling.

Morrison found what she had been searching for. She picked up a short stub of a candle, about an inch long. She stepped away from the rags and lit the candle. Then she gently set the candle stub down on the table in the center of the gas-soaked rags.

"Please—" Deena begged. "Please don't do this!"

And then Chuck and Jade were pleading too. All three of them begging desperately, watching the candle's flickering glow.

Linda Morrison acted as if she didn't hear their

pleas. "When this candle burns down," she announced, "it will set the gasoline on fire. There's so much junk in this basement that the whole place ought to go up like a torch."

"Please! Please don't!" Deena begged, sobbing.

"You won't suffer long," Morrison replied coldly.

She quickly made her way up the stairs and closed the door behind her.

They were alone now. Alone in the dark, except for the lone dancing candle flame.

Deena stared at the flame as if it were the center of the entire world. Its flickering light made the rags piled around it appear to be moving. The smell of gasoline hovered heavily in the air.

"We—we're going to burn to death!" Jade sobbed.

"Stop it, Jade!" Chuck ordered. "We're not dead yet. Let's think!"

"Think? There's no time to think!" Deena cried. "The candle is only an inch tall. As soon as it burns down, this whole place will burn like crazy!"

"Think," Chuck repeated. "Think. Think."

"I—I have an idea," Jade stammered. Maybe one of us can wiggle over there, stand up somehow, and blow out the candle."

Deena studied the distance across the basement. With their ankles tied together and their hands bound behind their backs, it could take hours to wriggle to the worktable. By that time . . .

"Too dangerous," Chuck said sharply. "There's too

much chance of knocking the candle over and setting the rags on fire."

"Can we wriggle up the stairs?" Deena wondered out loud.

"I—I don't think so," Jade replied in a shaky voice. "It's so far and—"

"Wait!" Chuck cried. "I see something."

He struggled away from the wall, scooting toward the center of the room.

Squinting hard, Deena saw what he was after—a twisted piece of metal. She felt the excitement of hope as Chuck backed up to the metal. He grabbed it in one hand and awkwardly began sawing it against the rope around his wrists.

"Hurry!" Deena urged. "Hurry! Is it cutting?"

"I can't tell," Chuck replied, working hard. "I can't see what I'm doing."

"Maybe I can help," Deena told him. She leaned away from the wall and scooted over to him.

"Let me try it," she told Chuck. She glanced down at the metal in his hands. It seemed to be a piece from an old door hinge. "It's not very sharp," she said.

"But is it sawing the rope?" Chuck demanded.

Deena examined Chuck's wrists. "No. No way," she murmured, unable to hide her disappointment. "It isn't working, Chuck."

"Hurry! Please hurry," Jade begged from against the wall.

"It isn't working," Deena told her with a sob.

"It's got to!" Jade cried. "The candle is almost burned down!"

Deena raised her eyes to the worktable.

Jade was right.

The candle had burned down to less than half an inch.

chapter
27

The candle had burned so low that its light was partly hidden by the rags piled around it. To her horror, Deena suddenly realized that it might ignite the rags even *before* it completely burned down.

"I give up!" Chuck cried, rolling away from the metal hinge. "We've got to find some other way."

Deena sighed in despair. If Chuck was giving up, then there really *was* no hope.

"Let's try crawling out of here," Chuck suggested. "Maybe we can make it up the stairs in time."

Deena knew that was a desperate hope. There was no way they could get out of the basement in time.

She turned and saw that Jade was already moving across the floor.

But to Deena's surprise, Jade wasn't moving toward the stairs, she was heading for the burning candle.

"Jade—what are you doing?" Chuck cried in alarm. "The gas fumes could set it off at any minute. Stay away from there!"

"I know what I'm doing," Jade groaned. She was crawling like a caterpillar, throwing out her feet, then pulling along the upper part of her body.

"Jade, stop!" Deena cried. "It's too dangerous!"

Jade ignored her and kept squirming. She struggled over to Farberson's body.

"Jade—what are you *doing?*" Deena cried.

She watched Jade shudder in horror. Then Jade straightened her legs and began pushing at Farberson's body, shoving it with both feet.

"He's too heavy," Jade grunted. She shifted, and planting her feet against Farberson's shoulder, pushed again.

Farberson's body slumped heavily onto its side. The blood-spattered saw came into view.

Jade paused for a moment, took a deep breath. Then she turned her back—and began to rub the rope on her wrists across the sharp teeth of the chain.

"Ohhh." Deena felt sick.

The saw bounced against Farberson as Jade pulled the ropes across it. Farberson's head then bumped heavily against the floor.

"It—it's working!" Jade stammered. "I can feel the rope—*Ow!*"

"Careful!" Chuck cried, struggling toward her.

"I'm free!" Jade announced. She raised her arms, pulled her hands apart. The rope slid off. She bent quickly to untie her feet.

Then Jade got up unsteadily. "Ow. My legs are asleep." She bent over Chuck and frantically started to untie his ropes.

Deena glanced up at the candle.

It had burned so far down that all she could see was the top of the flame.

"Jade—forget the ropes. Go blow out the candle!" Deena cried.

Jade lurched toward the workbench.

Not in time.

They all heard the loud *whoosh*.

chapter

28

The rags flared like a bright yellow fireball. As Deena gaped in horror, the top of the workbench blazed up.

Jade frantically untied Chuck. Then they both darted over to Deena to untie her.

As they worked, Deena stared past them at the workbench. The workbench was smothered in flames now, the fire climbing the wall.

Deena could feel the heat. She knew that at any moment the whole basement could go up.

Could they get to the stairs before the stairs burst into flame?

Chuck tugged the ropes off Deena's ankles. She struggled to stand up. But her legs had also fallen asleep. She grabbed on to Chuck.

"Hurry!" Jade cried. She ran toward the stairs.

Holding on to Chuck, Deena followed Jade.

A carton flared. The one above it burst into flame.

Deena choked on the thick smoke that blanketed the low room.

Up the stairs now. Her legs still weak and rubbery. Up the dangerous stairs, the fire crackling all around them.

Deena watched as Jade turned the knob. Watched her push against the door. Try the knob again. Push.

Then Jade turned back to them, her face twisted in horror. "The door—it's locked!" she wailed. "That woman locked us in. We're going to die!"

chapter
29

*T*hick black smoke billowed up the stairwell. Deena's eyes began to tear. She gasped for breath.

"We've got to break down the door. It's our only chance." Chuck and Deena stood next to Jade on the landing. "On the count of three, we ram the door with our shoulders," Chuck instructed. "Ready? One, two, three . . ."

Their bodies hit the door with a single heavy blow. The old wood made a cracking sound as it split.

Chuck shoved once again, harder. The door fell apart.

Chuck pushed through the opening. Then he helped pull Jade and Deena out.

As they staggered, coughing and choking, into the

kitchen, an explosion from the basement rocked the house. A hot blast of air hurtled the three of them across the kitchen floor toward the back door.

Deena gratefully stumbled out into the wind-driven sleet and ice. *I'm out,* she told herself. *We're all going to be okay.*

Lowering her head against the storm, she led the way around the house and down the driveway. At the street they turned back—in time to see the house erupt in flames.

Then, over the crackling of the fire and the steady drumming of the frozen sleet, they heard a distant wail, the wail of sirens—fire engines on the way to end the horror—forever.

"Another slice, anyone?" Jade opened the pizza box and pushed it to the center of the coffee table.

"Not for me," Deena groaned. "I'm stuffed."

"Is there any pepperoni left?" Steve asked.

"Hey, quiet, everyone!" Chuck ordered. "This is the part my film instructor told me about. Watch!"

The four leaned toward the TV, where an old Alfred Hitchcock movie was playing. "See where the plane's chasing him?" Chuck instructed. "That scene has been copied in dozens of other movies."

"Some old movies are pretty cool," Jade said.

"Do they have American movies you can rent in Australia?" Deena asked Steve.

"Of course we do. But they add kangaroos to all the movies!" Steve joked.

"Watch this part, guys," Chuck continued. He stared intently at the screen, leaning forward on the couch.

Deena sat back and watched the movie. Chuck is totally into this movie course he's taking at Madison College, she thought.

Deena still couldn't believe Chuck had decided to settle down for a while in Shadyside. But ever since they had escaped from the Farberson house six months earlier, he had become calmer, less wild.

Maybe the close call really scared him, she thought. Or maybe he just wants to stay close to Jade.

After Linda Morrison's trial, Farberson's insurance company had given Deena, Jade, and Chuck a reward. Deena's parents put her and Chuck's share in a college fund, which was now paying for Chuck's courses at Madison.

"Someday I'm going to make a movie about the Farberson murders," Chuck announced when the tape had ended.

"Are you kidding?" Jade cried. "No one would believe it."

"The way I'll make the movie, they'll believe," Chuck boasted. "You'll see."

"I still don't know much about what happened," Steve said. "Deena never wants to talk about it. Is it true the whole thing started with a phone call?"

"That's right." Deena sighed. "We were calling people at random. You know. Just as a joke. And Chuck—"

"Here. Let's try one," Chuck said. "Let's make a funny call. For old times' sake." He reached for the phone and raised the receiver to his ear.

"No way!" Deena shrieked. Furious, she grabbed the phone from Chuck's hand.

"Just joking!" Chuck declared. "Just joking, Deena."

Was he just joking? Deena wondered as she slammed the receiver back down. She stared hard at him.

Was he joking? Hard to tell, Deena decided. But she didn't like the mischievous grin on his face. She didn't like it one bit.

**Go back to where it all began!
Get the whole terrifying story—read
*THE WRONG NUMBER.***

About the Author

"Where do you get your ideas?"

That's the question that R. L. Stine is asked most often. "I don't know where my ideas come from," he says. "But I do know that I have a lot more scary stories in my mind that I can't wait to write."

So far, he has written nearly fifty mysteries and thrillers for young people, all of them bestsellers.

Bob grew up in Columbus, Ohio. Today he lives in an apartment near Central Park in New York City with his wife, Jane, and fourteen-year-old son, Matt.

THE NIGHTMARES NEVER END . . . WHEN YOU VISIT

Next: *TRUTH OR DARE*
(Coming in February)

It should have been fun. Seven teens on a ski weekend up in the mountains. But then a blizzard hit, ruining their plans. Now they're snowbound, with nothing to do.

So someone suggests they play Truth or Dare. An innocent game, they think. Who will tell the truth? Who will take a dare? And how far will they go?

But the game goes too far. One of them, it seems, would rather kill than tell the truth.

L.J. SMITH

THE
FORBIDDEN GAME TRILOGY

A boardgame turns dangerous when the teenage players are trapped inside and stalked by a bizarre supernatural force.

VOLUME I: THE HUNTER ......87451-9/$3.50
If he wins, she's his forever more....

VOLUME II: THE CHASE ....87452-7/$3.50
He's back - and coming to claim her at last!

VOLUME III: THE KILL ....87453-5/$3.50
Step into the Devil's playground....

And Look for the New L.J. Smith Trilogy...
DARK VISIONS, Vol. 1: The Strange Power
................87454-3/$3.50

All Available from ArchwayPaperbacks
Published by Pocket Books

Simon & Schuster Mail Order
200 Old Tappan Rd., Old Tappan, N.J. 07675
Please send me the books I have checked above. I am enclosing $_____ (please add $0.75 to cover the postage and handling for each order. Please add appropriate sales tax). Send check or money order-no cash or C.O.D.'s please. Allow up to six weeks for delivery. For purchase over $10.00 you may use VISA: card number, expiration date and customer signature must be included.

Name _____

Address _____

City _____ State/Zip _____

VISA Card # _____ Exp.Date _____

Signature _____ 964-05

FEAR STREET®

R.L. Stine

☐ THE NEW GIRL..............74649-9/$3.99
☐ THE SURPRISE PARTY....73561-6/$3.99
☐ THE OVERNIGHT.............74650-2/$3.99
☐ MISSING.......................69410-3/$3.99
☐ THE WRONG NUMBER.....69411-1/$3.99
☐ THE SLEEPWALKER.........74652-9/$3.99
☐ HAUNTED......................74651-0/$3.99
☐ HALLOWEEN PARTY........70243-2/$3.99
☐ THE STEPSISTER.............70244-0/$3.99
☐ SKI WEEKEND.................72480-0/$3.99
☐ THE FIRE GAME..............72481-9/$3.99
☐ THE THRILL CLUB............78581-8/$3.99
☐ LIGHTS OUT...................72482-7/$3.99

☐ THE SECRET BEDROOM.....72483-5/$3.99
☐ THE KNIFE......................72484-3/$3.99
☐ THE PROM QUEEN............72485-1/$3.99
☐ FIRST DATE....................73865-8/$3.99
☐ THE BEST FRIEND.............73866-6/$3.99
☐ THE CHEATER.................73867-4/$3.99
☐ SUNBURN......................73868-2/$3.99
☐ THE NEW BOY.................73869-0/$3.99
☐ THE DARE......................73870-4/$3.99
☐ BAD DREAMS ....78569-9/$3.99
☐ DOUBLE DATE ....78570-2/$3.99
☐ ONE EVIL SUMMER ....78596-6/$3.99
☐ THE MIND READER......78600-8/$3.99
☐ WRONG NUMBER 2......78607-5/$3.99

FEAR STREET SAGA
☐ #1: THE BETRAYAL.... 86831-4/$3.99
☐ #2: THE SECRET.........86832-2/$3.99
☐ #3: THE BURNING.......86833-0/$3.99

SUPER CHILLER
☐ PARTY SUMMER......72920-9/$3.99
☐ BROKEN HEARTS.....78609-1/$3.99
☐ THE DEAD LIFEGUARD
............86834-9/$3.99

CHEERLEADERS
☐ THE FIRST EVIL.........75117-4/$3.99
☐ THE SECOND EVIL....75118-2/$3.99
☐ THE THIRD EVIL.........75119-0/$3.99
☐ THE NEW EVIL............86835-7/$3.99

99 FEAR STREET: THE HOUSE OF EVIL
☐ THE FIRST HORROR ....88562-6/$3.99
☐ THE SECOND HORROR........88563-4 /$3.99
☐ THE THIRD HORROR...............88564-2/$3.99

Simon & Schuster Mail Order
200 Old Tappan Rd., Old Tappan, N.J. 07675
Please send me the books I have checked above. I am enclosing $____ (please add $0.75 to cover the postage and handling for each order. Please add appropriate sales tax). Send check or money order–no cash or C.O.D.'s please. Allow up to six weeks for delivery. For purchase over $10.00 you may use VISA: card number, expiration date and customer signature must be included.

Name _____

Address _____

City _____ State/Zip _____

VISA Card # _____ Exp.Date _____

Signature _____

739-17

RICHIE TANKERSLEY
CUSICK

□ *VAMPIRE*...70956-9/$3.99
  It's the kiss of death...

□ *FATAL SECRETS*..70957-7/$3.99
  Was it an accident--or was it cold-blooded murder?

□ *BUFFY, THE VAMPIRE SLAYER*...................79220-2/$3.99
  (Based on the screenplay by Joss Whedon)

□ *THE MALL*...70958-5/$3.99
  Someone is shopping for murder!

□ *SILENT STALKER*.......................................79402-7/$3.99
  *Terror is her constant companion as death
  waits in the wings...*

□ *HELP WANTED*...79403-5/$3.99
  *The job promised easy money -- but delivered
  sudden death!*

□ *THE LOCKER*...79404-3/$3.99
  Is someone reaching for help--from the grave?

□ *THE DRIFTER*...88741-6/$3.99
□ *SOMEONE AT THE DOOR*.........................88742-4/$3.99

Available from Archway Paperbacks

Simon & Schuster Mail Order
200 Old Tappan Rd., Old Tappan, N.J. 07675
Please send me the books I have checked above. I am enclosing $_____ (please add $0.75 to cover the postage
and handling for each order. Please add appropriate sales tax). Send check or money order--no cash or C.O.D.'s
please. Allow up to six weeks for delivery. For purchase over $10.00 you may use VISA: card number, expiration
date and customer signature must be included.

Name _____

Address _____

City _____ State/Zip _____

VISA Card # _____ Exp.Date _____

Signature _____ 733-07